Scar

CH

Scar

Margo

URBAN BOOKS

www.urbanbooks.net

Urban Books, LLC
300 Farmingdale Road, NY-Route 109
Farmingdale, NY 11735

ISBN 13: 978-1-945855-49-8
ISBN 10: 1-945855-49-5

First Trade Paperback Printing October 2018
Printed in the United States of America

10 9 8 7 6 5 4 3 2 1

*This is a work of fiction. Any references or similarities
to actual events, real people, living or dead, or to real
locales are intended to give the novel a sense of reality.
Any similarity in other names, characters, places, and
incidents is entirely coincidental.*

Distributed by Kensington Publishing Corp.
Submit Orders to:
Customer Service
400 Hahn Road
Westminster, MD 21157-4627
Phone: 1-800-733-3000
Fax: 1-800-659-2436

This book is dedicated to one of the strongest women I know.

My mother. I love you!

Chapter One

Tineya's Story

February 21, 2007

"All right now, Tineya. G'on up there in your room. You done had your li'l birthday party. You got a few li'l nice gifts. And all your li'l friends are gone. It ain't nothing but a bunch of grown folks down here! But before you go, come give me a kiss."

It was my twelfth birthday. I shouldn't have even been surprised, because in the hood it was like an unwritten rule that the kid's party usually turned into an adult party after a while. Although I didn't want to go upstairs to my room, I knew better. That was an argument that would end with me on the floor. If there was one thing my mama and daddy didn't play about, it was sitting up in grown folks' faces. Oh, and talking back. Wait, they didn't play about a lot of things.

I began to look around the kitchen. My eyes landed on the dish drainer holding the Pyrex measuring cup. My mother lived and died by the Pyrex brand of measuring cups.

"Hey, Ma, why do you like the Pyrex brand so much?"

"Little girl, stop playing with me."

Okay, of course she knew I was on my usual bullshit, just trying to prolong my stay downstairs.

"You know why I like Pyrex. It's sturdy. It can be used for wet and dry ingredients. Or at least, I will use it for both."

I just sat watching my mom go on about a measuring cup. Would you believe me if I told you how Ms. Tina's eyes would light up when she talked about anything concerning baking?

"I remember when I was a little girl my mama threw it at my drunk-ass daddy and it didn't break. That's when I knew that was a real measuring cup."

My dad and I burst out laughing at how goofy my mom really was.

"Man, Tina, how does your mom—may God bless her soul—and her violent past equate to the durability of a Pyrex?"

"'Equate? Durability?' Nigga get a pharmaceutical degree and don't know how to act."

"Oh, baby, I'm east side 'til I die." My dad twisted up his left hand, and his fingers formed the letter E. I couldn't stop laughing, messing with Nick and Tina. "But yo' ass still ain't answered my question."

She shrugged her shoulders. "Shit, I don't know. I knew the motherfucker was sturdy."

"Man, Daddy, she always tell a new interesting fact about that darn Pyrex."

Before I knew it, I was ducking a spatula that was flying at my head. "Watch yo' damn mouth. 'Darn' is too close to 'damn,' damn it." Her lips were pressed in that tight, straight line all mothers typically do to show that they're serious. "And you not slick! Take yo' ass upstairs."

I could only put my head down laughing. It was true I was trying anything to prolong my stay downstairs. I really had no reason to stay downstairs though.

I can get another piece of cake!

I smoothly cut myself another piece of cake. I sat there taking small stabs at the fluffy, moist piece of my birthday cake. My mom made me a yellow sheet cake with whipped buttercream icing. The icing was whipped to perfection. And I wasn't just saying that because my mom made it. She'd taught me to taste each ingredient. Even at a young age, I could pinpoint if something was off or missing.

See, my mother was a hairstylist by profession but a baker at heart. She made birthday cakes for all of the kids around our hood and the surrounding areas. She did the kind of baking that would make you forget about any problems you had, leaving you to focus only on the baked goods Ms. Tina created. And she wasn't out to break these families. She always showed love. Sometimes even if the parents didn't have the money to pay her, she would label the cake a birthday present. We would always bake all kinds of goodies together, and my birthday was no exception. In fact, it put emphasis on what she baked. Shit was crazy. I thought you could taste the love she put into baking her masterpieces.

So, I simply rolled my eyes, making my way to do just what she asked. Embarrassment wasn't on the menu on the night of my birthday, so I decided to keep any and all comments to myself. Hell, I made sure she didn't catch me rolling my eyes either. Respect was just a big part of my household. Even in a disagreement, my parents respected each other. That's not to say that things never got ugly, but they made sure I barely saw the ugly part.

"Damn, Tina. You just talk a million words a minute." My daddy came, adding his two cents. It was true my mom could talk with best of them.

"Shut up. The people from her birthday party just left ten minutes ago."

"Shit, that was ten minutes too damn long!"

"You better leave my baby alone."

"Shit, I'm just keeping it real!"

I could only smirk, because my dad always came to my rescue. When it came to me, he would always attempt to take the sting out of things unless it was serious. Nick and Tina always talked like best friends but bickered back and forth like they were brother and sister. They would flirt with each other like they just met. But when it came to holding each other down, there was no question the lengths they'd go to protect each other, like lions protecting their mate. They were both strong-willed. So it was sometimes interesting to see because nobody backed down. I didn't know what went on the streets, but my daddy gave my mama respect and vice versa. Long story short, Mama ran our house. No debate.

"Girl, go ahead on. My Tineya baby just had a dope-ass party! We just unburied the dead, better known as the Legacy Continues Jordan 5s." He exaggerated by using his hand to wipe the side of right shoe. "My baby is popping!"

I could only laugh at my parents' lingo. It was so nineties. I took that opportunity to take in my dad's attire. Mr. Nick was about six foot three in height. His weight I couldn't tell you, but he wasn't small by anybody's definition, that much I knew. He was dressed in simple black slacks with creases straight down the middle, paired with the white starched shirt that looked to be straight from the cleaners. No matter how many times I told him nobody wore creases anymore, he did. On his feet were the same shoes he'd gotten me for my birthday. Well, he bought them a month prior. So technically they were brand new since it was the first time he stepped his feet into the shoes.

My dad Nick was a sneakerhead before I even knew what it meant. Shoes were something that he took major pride in. Michael Jordans were at the top of his food chain. Sure, he wore other shoes. He was into restoring and stocking up on Michael Jordans though. His infatuation with sneakers had been pushed on both Tina and me. While I embraced and welcomed the love of sneakers, Tina did not. She would only wear certain brands. While she respected the sneakers, she was still more on the girly girl side when it came to fashion. You know, makeup, dresses, and heels made up the majority of her attire at the time.

"What you laughing at, little girl?"

"I'm laughing at my old parents' lingo. Nobody says that anymore! Y'all up here talking about 'dope' and 'popping.' Y'all old."

"No, she didn't! Nick, she turns twelve and think she grown! You ain't even a teenager yet. Slow ya roll, li'l mama!" my mama retorted jokingly, looking toward my daddy.

"See, Mama? You calling somebody 'li'l mama.' And, Daddy, why you got on them gym shoes with your granddaddy pants?" We had an ongoing joke about how Nick dressed. See, Nick would sometimes wear his slacks with sneakers like it was nothing.

He was a pharmacist with his very own pharmacy. He'd been in business for two years, so he needed to dress the part. As a family, we were all proud of him. In Detroit, he could've taken the easy way out. In the city, the wrong thing is the easiest thing to do. That's not to say Nick did everything right, but he took his wrongs, making them right.

Growing up, Nick had seen a problem. The problem haunted him in his dreams. It was a problem that no young man ever wants to see: his mother, helpless. His mother was sick, and he couldn't help her. She was diagnosed with cancer at a young age, even before Nick was born. Although that was a huge problem, an even bigger problem was the trouble she'd have to go through each month to get her medicine.

A lot of her medicine was a mix of uppers and downers, unfortunately. In the hood, some people used them as recreation drugs, making the medicine harder to access. Some days they would have to drive around to different pharmacies, trying to find certain medications. Then the insurance companies could see that certain medications were coming from different locations, causing a red flag. Nick had to see his mother go without her medicine for one reason or another, and he decided to do something about it. Nick decided to put in work, but not just how you probably think. He went to school.

He became a pharmacist. His mother lived until a week after his acceptance into pharmacy school. So, that added even more fuel to the fire of anger and the nagging feeling of hopelessness that burned through his body. He fought against the desire to just continue to make fast money. Nick created a small pharmacy in the city of Detroit. Nick had seen a problem and created a solution in an effort to help a community that was long forgotten.

"Hell nah! She got us messed up, baby." He looked at Tina with a shocked expression. Then he looked at me with a fake hurt face. "You know I was running late at the pharmacy. You know that when I'm working all the patient needs to see is my top half. Button-up shirt, lab coat, and my slacks. They can't see my feet. Besides, I couldn't fully match you. So at least we match by the feet. You better get hip." Nick paused as if something clicked in his head. "Oh shit, let me put these scripts up."

Nick

The prescriptions were a hot commodity. They're what every criminal wanted to get ahold of. With a prescription pad and a doctor's signature, a drug dealer could flood the streets with all types of narcotics. Since Nick's pharmacy was in the hood of Detroit's east side, he would bring the scripts, new and old, home with him in a locked briefcase. If a break-in were to happen, the intruder wouldn't get away with everything. It was system he used when he was still in the streets: never keep money and drugs in the same spot!

Even though Nick's goal was to place businesses in the areas nobody cared about, he still had to be smart. And he had an advantage. He knew the hood like the back of his hand. These were the very streets he grew up in. Same game, different players. Just because his motives were good, that wouldn't stop the scammers, deceivers, and robbers from lurking in the shadows. He couldn't be naïve about where he came from. Detroit was a lot of things. It was a city where some people would take from the next man instead of creating and working toward their own goals. Tupac said something about that in *Poetic Justice*. Basically, he said a man might downplay another man in an effort to make himself look better. You're simply mad because someone else is trying to better his situation and you ain't trying. As bad as it sounds, there are plenty of people with this fucked-up mindset.

Nick ran off to the basement with his briefcase in hand. He was heading to a wall safe he had built behind the furnace in the basement. Nick discussed many things with his girls, business moves included. He didn't want to force Tineya to become a pharmacist just because that was the path he chose, but he wanted her to know how his business was run.

Very few people knew how he ran his business: two pharmacy technicians, Tina, Tineya, and his brother, Nathan, to a certain extent. He even tried to teach Nathan the business, but that didn't work out. However, nobody outside his household, the people he trusted most, knew where he stored the scripts. Nick didn't necessarily want his family at risk. On the other hand, he didn't want to risk his family not being informed either. Ignorance was not bliss. At least, Nick didn't think so.

Tineya

"Grown men dress accordingly," Nick continued, coming up the basement steps.

I sat there and rolled my eyes dramatically, knowing that he was about to give a speech.

"The eighties and nineties were the best time! History is just repeating itself, baby. It's a never-ending cycle. Come on, baby, come dance with me!" My dad grabbed my mama with one hand, holding his forty-ounce in the other, while they did their rendition of a two-step, leaving me and the few friends they still had over laughing.

It was funny seeing my dad suited and booted with his lab coat in one hand and a forty-ounce of beer in the other hand. That was one of the many things I adored about him though, his humble spirit.

"Aye, baby girl, turn up that radio for your old man on your way up. Happy birthday! Daddy loves your pretty self. You're the only one your mom comes second to!"

My mom just kept dancing with a smirk and a wink. "I'll gladly take that position!"

Even I couldn't help but blush. My parents were the best to me. Maybe I was a little biased, but the love they showed me was incomparable. I grew up seeing so many mothers jealous of the father-daughter relationship. Or vice versa. Not my parents though. I was the most important person in their world collectively and separately. It was all love.

I simply turned up the radio like my dad requested. To my dad, Tupac sat at the top of the rapping food chain.

I couldn't help but start rapping along with Tupac's "If I Die 2Nite" as I made my way up the stairs to my room: "I'm sick of psychotic society. Somebody save me. Addicted to drama so even Mama couldn't raise me."

"Ahhhhhh!"

"Ughhh!"

A hard scream and something like a grunt woke me up from my sleep. I immediately recognized the voices belonging to my mother and my father. The scream shook my twelve-year-old body. I didn't know what to do, so I lay in my bed for a couple more seconds, taking deep breaths and trying not to let fear consume my body. The strong smell of cigarette smoke invaded my nostrils. It was so strong I got the sense that the person was a habitual smoker.

My parents don't even allow smoking in the house! Something is not right.

"Fuck, man, don't do this!"

It was like my daddy's voice snapped me out of a trance. His tone of voice wasn't one I'd ever heard. I just knew I needed to help. If I didn't know before then, at that moment, I knew for a fact something was wrong. I listened to different footsteps trample through the first level of our small house. It sounded to me like all the people were walking in the living room. So I decided to go the back way down the stairs so that it would place me in the kitchen, next to their bedroom. I didn't know what I was going to do, but I knew I couldn't just sit idle while my parents sounded like they were in distress.

"Look, man, g'on and do whatever you want to me, man. Leave my woman out of it. I told you, ain't nobody else in here." My dad's voice was so loud it was almost as if he was trying to tell me to stay put or hide. His voice was almost pleading, and my dad was not a pleading man. He said shit, and the shit got done. This shit right here was serious. I peeked around the door, into their room.

"I'll do whatever I want to do to this woman. She's fine, too." The intruder went to the chair Tina was bound to, and he rubbed all four tips of his fingers up against her arm. "You ain't in charge, homeboy. This my show. Now, where the fuck is the money?"

"I ain't got no fucking money! I ain't no fucking dope-boy. I don't deal in cash. Money goes to the bank in my business." In a matter of seconds, it was like Nick went to feeling irritated that the man would think he just kept stacks of money stored in his home.

The intruder got closer to Nick's face, taking the gun and smashing it into his face. My daddy sounded as if he were gargling mouthwash, but I knew better. I watched as blood began to spill from his mouth.

"I see, nigga. Broke-ass muthafucka. But you see, that ain't the only reason I'm here. I'ma take all this shit up out this house though! While you at it, take all that jewelry off them. Y'all wasted my time with this shit."

Hearing that made me drop my chin to my chest. Nick put his blood, sweat, and more blood into TNT Pharmacy. It took him years to get licensed, find good, solid staff, and turn a profit. Not only that, but he also had to build relationships with big-name insurance companies. Once he turned a profit, he bought himself and my mother simple Rolex watches with their initials written in incon-spicuous spots. I knew that hurt my parents' hearts because they held them near and dear.

"Look, man, I'm telling you I ain't got shit, dog."

"Nigga, you said that already. But my homeboy here gon' find something in this bitch," he retorted, smacking around any piece of furniture he passed for emphasis. The homeboy he spoke of walked through the house as if it were his own. He moved around the house fluently. For a second, I wondered if he'd been there before. I couldn't see his face though, due to his hoodie seeming too big and his whole head drowning in it.

"Come on na, man, you scaring my lady," Nick said through clenched teeth. Tina's cries grew soft. Those tears were full of fear for sure. It almost seemed as if she was even more scared than before.

"Nigga, you think I give a fuck about you or your bitch?"

From where I was standing behind the door, I could see but couldn't be seen. The man began to walk away from my father, going toward my mother with a gun hanging loosely in his hand at his side. Hearing the conversation was one thing. I wasn't prepared for the sight. It was too much. My mom on the floor now screaming bloody murder. She wasn't worried about herself though. See, to know Tina was to know that she too put her family's needs above her own. And Nick was her family. In her eyes, I could see her worry for my dad. In his eyes was the same worry for her. Their love was apparent even during such a fucked-up time. Just seeing that made me hot with anger.

My dad jumped up looking crazed as he watched the robber point the gun directly in my mother's face. "Yo, you bitch-ass nigga! Get that fucking gun out her face!" Nick caught the man completely off guard. But he recovered quickly, spinning around with the gun now pointed in Nick's direction.

"Nigga, you running up?"

I couldn't take it. I didn't know what to do, but rage took over as I turned back to the kitchen and snatched the mixing bowl off the counter. I launched the bowl in the intruder's direction. I missed. The bowl shattered against the wall, totally missing the mark.

"What the fuck?"

I ran full speed, hopping on the back of one of the intruders. He snapped around with the gun pointing in my direction. I guessed I completely caught him off guard, because the gun dropped.

"Baby!"

"Tineya. Baby, no!"

I heard my parents screaming out to me, but I chose to ignore them. The anger I felt seeping through my pores far outweighed any amount of fear pumping through my heart. My heart was crushed seeing all the blood all over the living room. It was like I could feel pieces of my heart chipping away. In that moment nothing else mattered. This was heartbreak in its truest form. In most people's lives, their parents are typically their first loves. Truly, it's your first encounter with love. Mine were two of the strongest people I knew, so seeing them in such a vulnerable state was indescribable.

My tiny fist whaling on the side of this man's face did nothing to him. As hard as I was swinging, I was no match for the strength of what appeared to be a grown-ass man. It almost mirrored throwing peanuts at a brick wall and expecting it to shake, rattle, and roll. Nothing.

He tossed my body over his head, slamming me onto the floor as if I were light as a feather. But once again, he was a grown man. However, the amount of force the man used was excessive by anybody's definition. The way he threw my body off his back reminded me of when I roughly threw my doll on the ground. If I had known karma was lurking, I would've rethought that move. Crazy comparison, I knew, but I couldn't help the way my mind worked.

"Ughhh!"

I could only lie on the floor, groaning and trying to catch my breath. Watching my daddy's eyes roll into the back of his head as he tried his best to get to me was gut-wrenching. I looked at my mama. She seemed to be in the same position as my dad! I was scared and hurt. I just knew my parents' lives were coming to an end. I felt that shit. The air in the room was thick.

I watched as one of the two intruders left through the door without saying a word. Then I looked at the man who'd flipped me over. I took note of his light gray eyes through his ski mask. I didn't know what to do, so I begged for our lives.

"Please, sir, I won't tell. Just don't hurt me. Please let me get some help for them. I want to save them."

The man's gray eyes grew dark. He began to pace the floor. Then he stopped in front of me. "Fuck them!"

I watched as a slight smirk appeared on his face. A navy blue ski mask with specks of silver all over it covered his face. Almost as if he came up with a bright idea, he stopped midstep. He bent down, picking up a piece of the bowl I'd just broken against the wall.

"Aye, my man. That's my baby. My only baby girl. Don't do her like that. I'll take whatever you got for her," Nick pleaded.

"Be careful what you wish for," the man said. Then, right in front of me, he shot and killed both my parents.

I screamed out, but I didn't have any time to even register what was happening. He was coming toward me. As I saw him moving toward my face, I attempted to block him with my forearm. It was to no avail, because he grabbed my arm, moving it out of his way. He brought the thick piece of glass across my face quickly.

"Ahhhhhhhhh!" I screamed out, using both hands to cup my face. Blood instantly spilled over and between the cracks of my hands. I could feel my face split in two. As I tried to fold my body into the fetal position, he grabbed the same place he'd just cut, and I felt a blade slicing across my shoulder blade. My back stiffened. I gave up any fight my young body could possess. All I could think about was trying to get away. Using the tips of my shoes, I tried scooting up to put as much space as I could between me and my assailant. "Umphh!"

"You little bitch! Where you going?"

He grabbed the back of my pants and belt to pull me right back toward him. He still held the same piece of the mixing bowl in his hand covered in my blood. He used it, slicing across the lower part of my back and going across my hip.

"Ssssss." I gritted my teeth. The pain was becoming too much. I started to feel myself slipping out of consciousness. There was nothing left to do. I just closed my eyes.

I could still hear him. He stepped over me as if I were nothing. He stopped abruptly and turned to look at me, kneeling. The smell of cigarette smoke was still in the air and even more apparent on his breath.

"Sorry, li'l mama. It's all in a day's work. You were just in the wrong place at the wrong time. Something like a casualty of war!"

The sound of the two pair of footsteps showed no urgency as they left the house as if they were asked to be there. No remorse. No empathy.

This was the day Tineya died and Scar was born.

Chapter Two

Tineya

"Whew, Tineya. That was a lot."

"Don't I know it."

"However, you made an amazing breakthrough. It was heartbreaking, but this begins the process of healing yourself mentally."

I sat there attempting to ignore my therapist. I began to look everywhere but at her. I wasn't in the room myself either. It took a lot reliving a part of my life that I wanted to forget. Yet, I felt so many bouts of guilt. She caused the flood gates to open for the tears I'd tried my hardest to keep at bay.

"Dr. Jenn, tell me then why do I feel so guilty? I shouldn't be trying to forget my parents. Seems kind of selfish to me."

I glanced around at the other survivors in the room, and they mirrored me. Our scars were very different. Some were physical. Scratch that. All were physical. But this was about the mental wounds that the physical wounds caused. All of us were a bit fucked up mentally.

"Tineya."

"Scar works fine."

"The only reason you want everybody to call you Scar is because for some strange reason you act like you think it's your fault."

"So you're saying—"

"Tineya, please let me finish. You know we're all about respect in this place. Just hear me out. Okay?"

The stubborn part of me only allowed me to nod. Dr. Jenn smirked along with a couple people in the room.

"I want to be clear. I understand your story. You are not the cause of any of it. I don't have to know your parents to know that they wouldn't appreciate you living your life in guilt. Today is your birthday."

Gasps could be heard around the small room.

"Wait. But you said it's the anniversary of your parents' death," a girl with a prosthetic leg commented, connecting the dots. Her hand immediately cupped her mouth. I simply nodded while Dr. Jenn continued.

"As I was saying, today is your birthday. You're amazing. You have plenty going for yourself. The guilt that you are carrying will only hinder you. You should pick a nice way to honor your parents and move in a positive direction of healing."

"How can I live like a normal young woman, huh? I have the hideous remains of the horrific night all over my body. The worst scar is the shit on my face. Not being able to hide an imperfection just sucks. Even if I can hide a piece of it, I can't hide all of it. The older I get, the more frustrated I get. You know what? I've had enough for today." I walked away, wiping my tears while trying to gather all my things and push open the door.

Dr. Jenn stopped me. "I think you did exceptional today. Opening up takes a lot of courage, and you did that, sis!"

That got a chuckle from everybody. The joke couldn't stop the tears from falling. I pushed open the door so that I could get all the way through it, but somebody pulled as I was pushing, causing us both to smash into the door and drop the things that were in our hands.

"Oh shit."

"What the hell?"

We got ourselves together. Nobody apologized. We made eye contact. Both of us had tears in our eyes.

"Well," she said, "since you not trying to apologize, can you please point me in the direction of a"—she looked at a business card in her hand—"Dr. Jennifer Long?"

I smirked. "I guess I could." I pointed into the room.

She winked. I walked away.

Chapter Three

Aaliyah

"So, Aaliyah, please tell me what brings you here to see me today."

"My boyfriend thought it would be good for me to have an unbiased person to talk to."

"Sounds like you have a good boyfriend."

"Yeah. He'd lose his shit if he heard me calling him my boyfriend."

"Ha. I guess that is a degrading way to address a man. I'm assuming he's a man. Am I correct in this assumption?"

"Oh, he's all man."

"Oh, my. Okay. So, how about we start there. He seems like your happy place."

"He is, but he way we met was anything but happy. We met in a fucked-up way. The way we met is actually part of the reason I'm here. Things started to go bad after my mom died of cancer. My dad—Calvin is his name—couldn't handle it."

Calvin

"Shut the fuck up! That nigga is not going to know we did it!" Calvin kept trying to reassure Stephanie that they wouldn't get caught. They had just run off with Eron's and Jamal's sack. The two would be on some ruthless shit, especially when it came to their money. Calvin knew Eron and Jamal were coming. He just didn't know how soon. He figured that he might as well get high, like "Beam me up, Scotty," as high as he possibly could before they darkened his doorstep.

Stephanie came along after Calvin's wife, Andrea, died. She swooped in so quick it was almost genie like. Stephanie introduced crack cocaine to Calvin when he was in a very vulnerable state. She was now his get-high buddy, fuck buddy, and accomplice when he needed her to be. Their relationship would be admirable if they were not fucking crackheads, literally.

"Don't fucking yell at me! You know them niggas gon' come looking for their shit. They don't even fuck with crack that much. You know they are keeping track of their return."

"You sound dumb as fuck. It's all money, and they're keeping track of everything they have in the streets. Now shut the fuck up before you wake that bitch up. I want us to be good and high when we fucking her." The bitch Calvin referred to was his and Andrea's eighteen-year-old daughter. She wasn't always a bitch to him, but when his wife was murdered, his feelings for his only daughter died with her. Calvin felt that Andrea took his whole heart in her casket. He didn't even love himself.

Stephanie smiled. "You right, let's hurry up!" Stephanie was a sick, calculating individual even before she made crack a part of her life. The only way to describe Stephanie when she was high was inhumane. Stephanie was bisexual and jealous of Aaliyah. She felt that with Aaliyah around she would never have all of Calvin's love. She wanted Aaliyah's pussy, too. She didn't want anybody else to have Calvin's attention, including his own daughter.

The little bitch ain't my daughter, so she shouldn't be his daughter.

Calvin was an upstanding citizen until Stephanie got to him. She was a calculating, manipulative individual. She watched from afar as he and Andrea had the perfect little family. She wanted that, so she took it. It was just that simple and plain.

"Um, um, um." Stephanie always thought back to how she took Andrea out because she was in her way. It made her pussy moist. Andrea was a problem and always had been. They went to Denby High School together. Stephanie was such a petty bitch that she was still mad about something that took place in their high school years.

Stephanie was interested in Calvin in high school, but everybody knew that he only had eyes for Andrea. Stephanie made a vow early in life that she would get that bitch Andrea back, and that she did. Stephanie was in love with Calvin early. In high school, the only thing Calvin would let Stephanie do was suck his dick. Stephanie held on that one day she would become his woman.

She would watch the "perfect little family" from afar. Stephanie was ecstatic when she got wind that Andrea was dying of breast cancer. Andrea battled with cancer for five years. There were many ups and downs. Stephanie felt that there were far too many ups, so she waited for Calvin to go to work and Aaliyah to go to school, and she made a real smooth break-in. She was in and out in a matter of minutes.

Andrea lay in her hospice bed reading and waiting for her nurse to come. When she heard the door slam, she was sure that it was Nurse Betty, but the face and the gun that looked back at her surprised the hell out of her. Stephanie didn't say a word and didn't give Andrea a chance to say anything before she shot her in the chest.

"Here, bitch, damn! I been sitting here calling your fucking name! What the fuck are you thinking about?" Calvin questioned as Stephanie snapped out of her trance, and she reached for the pipe, eagerly hoping she didn't say anything out loud. They passed the drug back and forth until all of the rocks were gone.

"Come on!" Calvin said in a slow, slurred voice, but Stephanie heard him. They crept into Aaliyah's room slowly and quietly. Aaliyah lay on a twin mattress in the corner of the room on the floor. The bed lay against a raggedy headboard, with no box spring and no bed frame. Calvin never bought his daughter anything that would mean spending money that could be spent on getting high. They found the headboard on the way back from copping some crack, and it was grabbed for this occasion. Stephanie spotted the headboard and talked Calvin into carrying it home.

Today was Aaliyah's birthday. Happy birthday. Today was Aaliyah's Birthday, but she wasn't getting a present. She was giving away her most precious gift. They were taking the pussy. A woman never forgets about losing her virginity. Aaliyah would always remember the fucked-up beginning.

Calvin had grabbed a rope to tie her hands to the headboard. Stephanie was in a rush. She grabbed the rope and began to tie Aaliyah's arms to the headboard. Calvin couldn't wait. Calvin hadn't had any good pussy since Andrea died.

Shit, maybe her pussy will be just like her mama's. How does that saying go? Like mother, like daughter, right? Calvin's sick mind wondered. He began rubbing up and down on Aaliyah's thigh, causing her to stir in her sleep.

"What the fuck are you doing?" Aaliyah asked, jumping from her sleep.

Stephanie started to rub her hair. "Just relax, and this could be fun."

"Bitch, get yo' sick ass the fuck away from me before I fuck you up!" Aaliyah said as she snatched her head from Stephanie's touch.

Aaliyah was shocked. Her dad was many things, but she never thought he would fucking rape anybody let alone his own fucking daughter. Aaliyah was sure that that sick bitch Stephanie put the thought into Calvin's mind. Stephanie always made an excuse to bump into Aaliyah or to come walk in her room. They fought many times. Aaliyah always thought of running away, but where would she go? She knew the streets of Detroit would eat her alive. Calvin's house wasn't much, but it wasn't the Detroit streets either. They didn't call Detroit "the murder mitten" for nothing. Bitches was getting tied up and put in trunks. The Detroit streets were like no other.

Aaliyah started to squirm as she looked at Stephanie take her place between her legs.

"Come on, Stephanie, don't do this shit please."

Stephanie looked at Aaliyah dead in her eyes with a blank look, yet it was filled with desire as she began to lick her pussy. Aaliyah felt her blood boil. She just wanted to kill the sick bitch Stephanie. Every lick put Aaliyah's feelings in an uproar. She felt a wide range of feelings from disgust to nausea to anger to abandonment.

"Daddy, why are you letting her do this shit? What the fuck is wrong with you?" Aaliyah begged her daddy, but he was busy jacking his dick, plus the glazed look in his eyes let her know that there was no hope. He was on a crack binge.

If I get out of this, I swear to God I am going to kill these bitches. God forgive me. I can't let them get away with this shit. How could a father let this shit go down? I know my mama is rolling over in her grave at all of the fuck shit that I have been going through since her death. But this fuck shit right here takes the cake. Ever since my mom was taken from me, all I've known is suffering.

Aaliyah decided to just shut up. She refused to keep begging people who really didn't give a fuck about her.

They are probably getting off from me begging. I won't make this shit any easier for them.

Calvin went from rubbing his dick all over Aaliyah's face to trying to stuff it down her throat. Aaliyah just lay there, using her teeth to guard him from entering her mouth. Calvin was hurting his dick hitting it up against Aaliyah's teeth. He was shoving his dick so hard that it was causing his piss hole to spread.

"Open your fucking mouth before I punch you in it."

"Fuck you!" Aaliyah gritted her teeth as Stephanie finally came up for air.

"You know what? Fuck it. I want some pussy anyway."

"Taste good, too, Calvin."

I got to get the fuck out of here.

Aaliyah just wanted to scream at the top of her lungs. In Detroit, though, niggas minded their own business. Nobody would call the cops unless a body was found. Aaliyah had never felt so helpless. She knew her dad and Stephanie were fucked up, but this shit threw her for a loop. She stayed out of their way, so she didn't understand why they were fucking with her, literally. Females got raped every day. How many could say that their crackhead dad and his psycho crackhead bitch committed the ultimate betrayal?

Aaliyah knew exactly when she fucked up. When she realized that her dad was fucked up, she should've left. She fucked up when she thought that she could trust Calvin's crackhead ass. Crack took any and every piece of his heart and loyalty away. He wasn't loyal to anything but crack cocaine.

Aaliyah was shaken from her thoughts by Calvin trying
to break through her hymen. At this point Aaliyah was
numb, and her anger reached new heights.

"Ahhhhh! Ouch! Daddy, please stop it, dammit!" Aaliyah
literally heard her pussy ripping apart. It was almost like
Calvin was possessed. He couldn't hear her screams. He
was beating her pussy wall relentlessly. There was no
mercy for Aaliyah.

Aaliyah's voice was muffled by Stephanie slamming
her pussy smack dead into her mouth. Stephanie took
her pussy, grinding it hard against Aaliyah's mouth. The
pressure against her teeth was unbearable. Something in
Aaliyah clicked, causing her to lose it. She started shaking
really hard, trying to get them to get the fuck off of her.

Slam!

The janky headboard fell on top of all of them. Calvin
and Stephanie got hit the hardest because they were on
top of Aaliyah. Aaliyah felt her dad stop jerking, and the
bitch Stephanie fell off the side of the mattress.

Aaliyah was crying so hard. They were the silent,
deadly tears. She knew she needed to focus. There was
no way she was letting either of them live. Aaliyah looked
around, trying to figure out how she could get out of this
situation. Aaliyah noticed that the rope was coming from
up under the headboard rails. She wiggled and worked
the rope from up under the rails, using some unforeseen
strength to push her daddy and his girlfriend up off of
her. Aaliyah pushed them off her. Aaliyah finally stood
up, breathing deep, long, and hard. She was fuming and
shaking as she looked at the blood leaking between her
legs. Aaliyah marched to Calvin's closet where she knew
he kept his old-ass .40-caliber pistol.

Click, clack. Aaliyah put two in the chamber. She made
her way back to her room.

"Umm, what the fu . . ." Calvin didn't even finish because he was staring down the barrel of his own gun.

"Shut up, bitch!" Aaliyah hollered. She was now a cold, calculating woman. She didn't see Calvin as her father. She saw him for what he was, a fucking predator.

Boom. Boom! The shots rang out.

"I guess the job is done already."

Aaliyah snapped her head in the direction of the man's voice. She wasn't scared. She knew who the voice belonged to. It was Jamal. She had seen him in passing. He would always be nice to her. When Aaliyah would see him at the store or at a restaurant, her bill would magically be paid up. If she was in the mall, then whatever she was attempting to purchase would be paid for. It took Aaliyah a while to realize that he was the common denominator in all of these situations. He never stuck around to get acknowledged, nor did he expect anything in return.

He was also Eron's right-hand man. They sat at the top of the city together. The Detroit streets ran deep, and Eron and Mal ran right alongside some of the best hustlers Detroit had to offer. Aaliyah had a thing for Eron though. They were both hot commodities in the D, but Eron caught her eye. There was something about him that had her attention.

"I see," Eron replied, leaning on the doorframe.

"If you're looking for your drugs, they smoked it up!" Aaliyah announced, looking Eron dead in his eyes then shifting her glare without blinking to look at Jamal.

"Nah, I already knew that it was gone. I was coming to do something else, but it looks like somebody already beat us to the punch," Eron said. "Aye, Mal, do me a favor and call the cleanup crew. Let me help her get some of her shit together. I'll meet you in the car."

"Already on it." Eron noticed that the phone was already up to his ear as he walked away. The two really operated like brothers. People often thought they were. Between Eron and Mal, it was all love and loyalty. They moved in sync. It didn't matter who was in the lead because they always had each other's back. The shit was a given. Loyalty was their chosen lifestyle.

"Aye, put on some clothes. We got to get up out of here."

Damn, he is fine. Did I really kill them? Damn, he is fine.

"Yo! No time for spacing out. Come and put this shit on," Eron told Aaliyah as he started to snatch clothes off the floor, handing them to her.

Aaliyah finally came out of her loopy state. "Okay, I'm sorry." Aaliyah threw the clothes on as quickly as she possibly could.

Eron grabbed her hand, pulling her close and whispering in her ear, "I can just about piece together what happened, but when we get to where we're going, I'ma need you to fill in the blanks." Eron had no reason to pull her close, but as awkward as the situation was, he wanted her close to him. In all the sweat and downed state of mind he still saw all the beauty that Aaliyah possessed. Even in her vulnerable state, Eron was able to see and appreciate that Aaliyah was fine as hell.

"Okay!" Aaliyah replied as they rushed through the halls of her apartment building. She glanced back, noticing about five figures in all black rushing down the same hall that they had just come from. Eron grabbed her head, turning it toward him. "Quit being nosey! Come on! In this situation, the less you know, the better."

Aaliyah just listened to the man. They crossed the street and headed toward a black-on-black Yukon Denali. Aaliyah reached for the back door handle, but before she could grab it, Eron grasped her hand. "I got it!"

"Thanks!"

"Aye, bruh! You might want to hurry up. We need to get ghost!" Mal said, interrupting the stare down between Aaliyah and Eron.

Eron went to hop in the front seat. "Man, I got this! Even when I appear to be thinking of something else, I'm always thinking about the task at hand. Remember that. Dog, a nigga can multitask."

Mal laughed. "Yeah, okay, man, whatever you say. Where you want me to take li'l mama?"

"You can take us to Motor City."

"Oh, are you staying there with her?"

"Yeah. I'm sure Aaliyah doesn't want to be by herself."

Jamal looked at his brother with a knowing look. He knew Aaliyah was good as gone. He knew Eron was good as gone. It didn't even matter which way you put it. Aaliyah was a hell of a catch. It took a real nigga to look past the fucked-up life that was she was forced to live to see it. Both Jamal and Eron noticed it, but only one would act on it.

Aaliyah woke up to the bright Motor City hotel and casino lights shining in her face. Immediately she felt a rush of insecurities. *I don't even know these niggas! Maybe I should just take off running when he opens the door. Shit, but what do I have to lose? Did I just kill not one but two people? I just killed my daddy! Where the fuck would I run to anyway?*

Eron spoke up, reaching for Aaliyah's hand. "Come on, Aaliyah."

"Aye, how do you know my name?"

Eron made his way through the hotel lobby with Aaliyah in tow. He smirked. "You live in my city. What you mean how do I know you? I know the bums, cab drivers, even people who attempt to stay off the radar."

Eron left Aaliyah's mouth hanging open as he winked. "Now come on. We got a few things to clear up." Eron finished ushering them off the elevator to the room door.

Aaliyah was once again speechless by the sternness in Eron's voice. When he talked, your best bet was just to listen. He had a deep, authoritative voice. Eron wasn't the type of person who talked just to hear himself talk. He always said things with substance.

Eron opened the door. "I'ma run you some bathwater. That's our best bet right now. You should just soak in the water. That should help with some of the irritation. Maybe tomorrow I can take you to a clinic that I know of in Highland Park or some shit so you can get a test done, but we can't say anything about what happened at your dad's house. I mean, that fuck nigga Calvin's house. After what we talk about tonight, we forget about it. Got it? I know it won't be easy, but I promise you'll get through it."

"Okay," Aaliyah replied with her head down as she walked into the bathroom as Eron began to fill the Jacuzzi tub. The room was one that Aaliyah would've enjoyed under different circumstances. The room had decadent bedding with 300-thread-count linens. The bathroom had marble floors with a separate soaking tub and shower. There was even an in-room coffee maker featuring Starbucks coffee, and the minibar had an extensive selection. There was twenty-four-hour in-room dining, a business center, and a fitness center. The "Deluxe King" was the simplest room that the hotel held.

"We'll talk when you get out!" he said, making his way out of the bathroom.

Aaliyah immediately began to cry as she began to undress. The stress of her situation began to settle in. She didn't cry because she committed a double homicide. She cried about the misery that was called her life. Making her way into the tub, Aaliyah couldn't help but wonder what direction her life would go. Still in a state of shock, Aaliyah, with a surprisingly empty mind, lay back in the tub.

Knock, knock.
"Aye, are you going to stay in there all day?"
Aaliyah looked at the clock on the wall. "Damn, my bad. I didn't know a whole hour passed. Here I come."
Eron opened the door just as Aaliyah stood up in the tub to hand her some clothes that he had Mal buy so that he could dispose of her clothes. He was mad that Jamal only got her some nightclothes, so he had to figure out a way to get her something for tomorrow. There was no way she was about to be out in pajamas like the young ratchets. Eron didn't want to leave her side. He felt that too many people left Aaliyah when she needed them the most.
"Damn!" Eron fucked around and let slip out. Eron had seen her naked earlier, but there was dried-up blood coming from her vagina down her legs. Now he was seeing her in such a clean and pure state. It was kind of erotic.
Aaliyah stood there, stunned that she didn't even attempt to cover up. In such a weird situation, she still felt sexy under Eron's gaze. "Uh, um, so you just gon' stand there being a creep or nah?"
Eron chuckled. "Shit, I'm a man! Hurry up with your smart-ass mouth." Eron wasn't new to seeing a female's body, but that was something he would never want to get used to. He felt that a woman's body was like sculpted art. You couldn't tell Eron that Aaliyah's body wasn't molded specifically for him. In reality, it was only a ten-second look, but he used it to his full advantage. Eron took in her slender neck. He imagined his dick going down her

throat. His stare continued to make its way down to the areola of her breast to the inward dip of her waistline to the fullness of Aaliyah's hips.

Aaliyah stepped out of the tub, snatching the clothes from Eron's clutch.

"Okay! Can you get out?" Aaliyah said, pushing him out of the bathroom. Eron felt bad. He didn't want Aaliyah to feel like he was a creep, but shit, what was he supposed to do? At least he didn't say what he was thinking.

Aaliyah quickly got dressed so that she could get this dreadful talk over with. Aaliyah came out of the bathroom, noticing that Eron had taken his shirt off but not his pistol. The sight before her was sexy as fuck. He lay on the bed with his eyes closed. She took a moment to take in the man the streets called Eron.

Eron was six foot five and weighed 240 pounds, solid. He looked like he ate weights. Eron stayed in the gym. Regardless of anything, he always made time for the gym. He had light brown skin free of any sign of acne or blemishes. He had straight white teeth. He was anybody's definition of fine. Don't get it twisted though. He was far from a pretty boy. And his reputation in the streets was cutthroat, the opposite of him. It was ugly.

"All right, you can stop staring now. I just wanted to give you a peek since I got an eyeful," Eron said, laughing as he winked. "Now sit down. We got shit to talk about."

"Okay, so what do you want to know, man?" Aaliyah snapped.

"Look, come on now. You know what I want to know. I got shit I could be doing, bruh! I done took your problem and made it mine. So, dog, you need to get to talking, don't you think?"

Aaliyah rolled her eyes as she began to relive the fucked-up shit she had experienced earlier that day. She went all the way back to how they lived before her mom

died and crack became a part of her life. Aaliyah wanted
Eron to know that it wasn't always like this. She literally
watched her father's health, appearance, and love for
her decline all because his love for crack cocaine was
stronger. She didn't lose respect for her father because of
his drug use. She lost it because of how drugs turned him
into a monstrosity.

The entire time she talked, she looked down to the
floor. She didn't even notice the tears until she felt Eron's
hand wipe her face. Aaliyah was taken aback by the frown
on Eron's face. It was in contrast to the gentle touch of
his hand on her face.

"So that's my story." Aaliyah shrugged her shoulders.

"Don't feel too bad, Aaliyah. Everybody got a story to
tell. Look at it this way: you don't have to deal with it
anymore. Aye, I got one question for you though. How
do you feel about actually committing the murders? In
telling this whole story, you never once said that you
regret it or that you feel sorry. I mean, as fucked up as he
was, he was still your father."

Aaliyah looked up into Eron's eyes. "That's because I
don't. I don't feel any remorse."

As awkward as it sounded, at that moment Eron knew
that Aaliyah was the type he needed to keep close, but the
question was, how close?

"Doctor, are you with me?"

"Yes, I'm all ears. I see Eron is a big part of your story."

"He is. He has a lot to do with my growth. It's not all
good, but it damn sure ain't all bad. We've discussed so
many different things. He's definitely my best friend, as
cliché as that sounds. Hey, I have a question."

"Go right ahead."

"Can you explain a little bit more in depth about the
patient-therapist confidentiality clause?"

"You mean about the paper you signed?"

"Yes, is that a problem?"

"No, not at all. Patient-therapist confidentiality is serious. There're only a few reasons to break the confidentiality. Keep in mind those are extreme cases. A therapist may have to share the diagnosis in order to receive payment. Typically, those are for insurance patients. Since you're a cash patient, you don't have to worry about that. Next, if required by state or federal officials. Even then there has to be probable cause. Next, if the patient is endangering people who cannot defend themselves. This is usually in the case of children or the geriatric demographic. Lastly, if a patient is a danger to herself or others, then I have to contact the proper authorities. Is this reasonable to you?"

"Yes, absolutely."

"Okay, I just want to make sure you thoroughly understand that what we discuss will not be discussed at my leisure."

"I understand."

"Now that that's out of the way, do you want to continue?"

"Yes. I want to make sure I'm not just telling you senseless stuff."

"I want you to discuss anything that you want to get out."

"Okay."

"Continue."

"Now I get to wake you up," Aaliyah said, assuming that Eron wasn't up.

"Nope, li'l mama, you still late. I'm already up," Eron growled with sleep fully evident in his voice. "You ready to go to the doctor to get a checkup?"

"Yeah, I'm ready and waiting on you, slow man."

Eron's eyes finally snapped open. *Shit!* he thought. Eron took in Aaliyah's appearance. She had a real nigga smitten. He was at a loss for words. She was dressed simply in leggings and a T-shirt. He loved the simplicity of her appearance. Late last night, he had this little gutter bitch, Jessica, stop through and bring Aaliyah some comfortable clothes so that they could shoot some moves today. Jessica's face was, of course, all balled up, but she knew that she could easily be replaced. Jessica was who he and Mal used for road trips. She had the typical college-girl look down pat. Jessica could throw on her Ohio State hoodie, glasses, and her book bag and she would blend right on in.

"Yo, come back down to earth," Aaliyah said, laughing because she knew that he approved of her appearance. It made her feel good that he was even staring at all. He was the type of nigga who made every woman want his attention.

"Shut up! Let me jump in the shower real quick," Eron said, frowning as he made his way to the bathroom. He didn't like it one bit that she had him speechless, and she knew it.

Aaliyah sat on the bed, just thinking about the reality of her situation. She was even worried about the fact that she had nobody else in her corner. What would she do for money? What would she do about finishing school? She only had a couple of months left before she would be done. Where would she live?

"Damn!" Aaliyah said just as Eron was coming out of the bathroom.

"Are you in here going crazy? Are you talking to yourself, Aaliyah?"

"Man, I just . . . I don't know." Aaliyah was so flustered. Not knowing your next move would have even the best in the same state of mind. "I don't have shit. I don't know anything right now. I hate this feeling. I blame my daddy."

"Stop calling that nigga yo' daddy. Daddies don't do the shit that nigga did to you. That nigga don't deserve the title."

"But it wasn't always like that. He was a daddy before my mama died."

"So you really think that it's okay for him to stop parenting because his wife died? You don't think he has wanted to molest you?"

"Stephanie talked him into it."

"Man, what? The thought has to be there in order for him to actually go through with it."

"No, but—"

Eron cut Aaliyah off. "Nigga, ain't no buts! Not only did he violate you, he helped somebody else violate you. Look, man, if you are going to defend that nigga's actions, then don't do it to me. I don't ever want to hear that shit."

Aaliyah knew that what Eron was saying was true. She didn't even have a comeback. She knew that she sounded like a fool defending and making excuses for a man who raped her. He stopped being her father on that day. The day was her birthdate, to be exact.

Eron couldn't explain the warm feeling that was running through his body. He just felt that he wanted to protect Aaliyah. "Look, you straight. I want you to trust in me. Now, I know from your story that trusting won't be easy. But for whatever reason, I just want to help you. I want you safe. I'm not, excuse my language, a 'Captain Save-a-ho' type of nigga, but I know that you didn't deserve half the shit you have had to go through. Nah, I didn't make myself known, but Mal kept helping you. I see what he sees in you. You're one of the few diamonds in the rough. The hood has a way of chewing you up and spitting you out if you let it."

Aaliyah looked up at Eron, seeing the truth in his eyes. "You know, I wasn't always positive that Jamal was the person helping me. That's crazy. At the store by my house, the man would always tell me that my money was no good, and he would never tell me why."

"Yeah, I would ask why he did it. Mal explained to me who your dad was. Well, who that nigga Calvin was to you. We watched that nigga decline. Mal would always talk about how his daughter was the one suffering. At first, I was confused as to why the nigga cared so much. He's a lot of things, but caring ain't one of them. He wanted to help you, but he didn't want you to think he was looking for anything in return."

"Damn, remind me to give him a big hug. That's amazing. He was looking out and didn't even know me."

Eron looked at Aaliyah blankly. "Aye, you don't have to give that nigga a hug. You can just say something along the lines of, 'Aye, thanks for looking out for me.'"

Aaliyah busted out laughing. "No, I got to show him my appreciation."

"It doesn't take a hug to do it. You know your mouth works just fine."

Aaliyah grinned. "So you want me to use my mouth to thank him?"

Eron's face balled up immediately. "Nah, you know that's not what I was saying."

"Okay. So I'ma give him a church hug." Before Eron could interrupt, Aaliyah continued. "Okay, let's just get this over with." Aaliyah was just able to shake the solemn mood while Eron was in a daze walking behind her.

He couldn't help but wonder what exactly he wanted to do with this chick. Most women did exactly what he said, but this chick was actually going up against him. He didn't love it, but he loved the way she was willing to stand up for herself.

The duo made their way out of the hotel to the same black Yukon, only Eron hopped in the driver seat. Aaliyah assumed that it was his truck. She'd seen him around her hood. The two were lost in their thoughts as T.I.'s beats filled the air.

"I'ma take you to this little clinic in Highland Park. It's a real small, chill spot so you won't have to worry about the police getting involved. Then we'll have to go back to your house to make it seem like you're looking for your father, and we'll go file a police report."

"That makes sense. I was wondering how I would cover that."

"I told you I got you. Come on," Eron said in a reassuring tone as they hopped out of the car.

The sign read HIGHLAND PARK CLINIC, and it looked rough. The clinic was full of crying babies with young mothers and dopefiends nodding out. That's all Highland Park was though. It was a small city within Detroit. Detroit was far from being a suburban community, but Highland Park was a fucking warzone.

Eron walked in behind Aaliyah.

"What up, E?"

"Hey, E!"

"E, what's up?"

Aaliyah's head swiveled. People were sitting up straight in their seats like the principal had just come into the classroom.

"Aye, E man, can I holla at you outside?"

"Man, damn. Aaliyah, go ahead and sign in. Let me holla at dude right quick."

What Aaliyah didn't know was that Eron had a long-standing relationship with this particular clinic. This clinic was ghetto in every sense of the word, but it was actually a smart investment. The clinic had a pharmacy inside of it. Dr. Brown and Dr. Angelo, the duo who had offices here, were brothers. Dr. Brown was the pharmacist, and Dr. Angelo was the doctor. They took a liking to the young Eron.

Eron went into the clinic for a checkup and appro-ached Dr. Angelo with a proposition that he couldn't refuse. Dr. Angelo then took Eron into his office to get a better understanding.

"I hope you don't mind, but I'm paging my brother, who is the pharmacist here at the clinic."

"No, I don't mind. In fact, I'm sure he can benefit from this business proposition too."

In walked Dr. Brown, who was almost a replica of his older brother.

On that day, they sat down, negotiated numbers, and had been in business ever since. That was seven years ago. It was a smooth operation. Nobody but the three of them, including Jamal, knew their connection to each other. Eron would send people to the doctor to get "check-ups." Dr. Angelo would usually prescribe Xanax, codeine/promethazine, oxycodone, morphine, or Percocet. With this connect, Eron and Jamal were able to feed the streets without a problem.

Dr. Angelo and Dr. Brown loved the city. They just wanted to help the underprivileged. In doing so, they didn't get paid what a doctor should, because they accepted Medicaid, which most people on welfare had. Neither one of the men liked the idea of participating in illegal activities, but when they thought of the "American dream," they didn't think it would be this hard to help people. It was either sell out or start to make the poor have to pay higher copays. That was something they just didn't want to do. So, Dr. Angelo and Dr. Brown did what they thought was best.

They debated about the situation for a while. They both got good vibes from Jamal and Eron. In this business, you had to follow your first mind. Dr. Brown felt that Jamal and Eron were calculating individuals. They were not loud and obnoxious. They moved silently. Money was their motive. And the amount of extra income was astronomical.

Aaliyah attempted to sign in, but the lady at the desk immediately told her that she could step to the back. Aaliyah was buzzed into the office, where her weight and temperature were taken.

"What brings you in today?"

"I just need to be tested and get a Pap smear," Aaliyah mumbled. She wasn't too happy that they would have to touch around in her pussy, because it was very tender and sore, but it needed to be done. It was better to be safe than sorry.

"Okay, you can step to room four, and the doctor will meet you there. One quick question: you call yourself messing with E? 'Cause my friend Jessica is his bitch. You can't compete. Just thought you should know. Don't get too comfortable. He always goes back to her."

Aaliyah was taken aback by the chick's boldness. *Who is this bitch talking to?* Aaliyah smirked at the medical assistant as she turned around to look the bitch dead in the eyes. She didn't want baby girl to think a confrontation like this would ever happen again. Aaliyah was going to make sure that the medical assistant went back and told her friend that she was not to be approached in any form or fashion.

What she didn't know was that Eron stood on the other side of the door, listening to the exchange. He needed to see if she could handle herself. Weakness wasn't a trait he wanted in his camp. What he wanted to do with her, he wasn't sure, but he wanted Aaliyah safe around him. Eron listened closely from where he stood. He could even see the exchange, but he couldn't be seen.

"You got a lot of nerve. I'll give you that. You got some big-ass brass balls." Aaliyah was damn near in a full-fledged laugh. Aaliyah finally looked at the chick's nametag. "Robin! Let me teach you a thing or two. Don't come questioning me about a motherfucking thing." Aaliyah stepped closer to Robin. "I need you to feel these words that I am saying to you. With the night I had, I could end your shit right here and now. Think again before you step to me. Now, if you want it to be a problem, I'll gladly alleviate you of that problem by solving it. Now you tell me what you want to do."

Eron cleared his throat, making his presence known. "The doctor is ready for you in room four," Eron said, reaching for Aaliyah's hand.

Aaliyah didn't even acknowledge Eron. She maintained eye contact with Robin. Eron snatched Aaliyah's arm, pulling her into his chest.

"Aye, Robin, do me a favor. When you see her just go the other way. Feel me?"

"Yeah, E," Robin answered with her head down.

Eron led Aaliyah to her room. "Get undressed and urinate in the cup."

Aaliyah snatched the cup and went to the bathroom across the hall to handle that. She noticed Robin at the nurse's station. As soon as Aaliyah looked at her, she looked at the floor. She came back in the room still pissed about the confrontation with the cheap-ass medical assistant.

"Fix your face!"

"People checking me about you. I don't like that shit. I don't even fuck with you like that."

"You don't fuck with me huh? Not yet, but you will. Not on no conceited bitch shit, but women want to be close to me. They are not going to like you. That's some shit I can't control. I can stop them from approaching you though. I can assure you it won't happen again. The girl Jessica she was talking about, I fuck with her from time to time. It is not close to being anything serious. I haven't fucked with her in a while, which is why her homegirl felt the need to approach."

"I hear you!"

Aaliyah silently got undressed from the waist down, throwing the sheet over her legs. She wasn't sure if she was mad about the chick testing her or about Eron really having a woman. Even if the bitch wasn't his girl, she didn't want nobody close enough to him to feel like they could check the next bitch.

Dr. Angelo came in and said, "Hey, Ms. Aaliyah, I received your urine, so I'll run some tests. Do you have a secure e-mail or phone number that I can send the results to?"

"No, I—"

Aaliyah was cut off by Eron. "You can text my phone, Doc. She'll be with me anyway."

Aaliyah just nodded, agreeing with Eron.

She gon' be with me? Where did that come from? Eron thought.

Am I really going to be with him? Aaliyah thought.

Eron's and Aaliyah's thoughts ran rampant. Eron couldn't explain the chemistry between the two. Aaliyah felt that she had nothing to lose and that Eron was nothing short of a winner. She knew that she was a pretty girl, but to have Eron's attention you had to be a real woman. Not just a pretty face. Not just a nice body. Not just a bad bitch. You had to be a combination of those things.

"Okay, Ms. Aaliyah. We can make this fast. Would you like Eron to leave the room?"

"No, it's fine."

"Okay. Lean back and put each foot in the stirrups. It shouldn't hurt, but you will feel pressure."

Eron sat in the chair directly behind the doctor so he could see everything. The doctor put lubrication on the speculum before sticking it up Aaliyah's vagina then widening it. Dr. Angelo then used a long Q-tip-like utensil to scrape cells along the vagina wall to test for cervical cancer and sexually transmitted diseases.

Aaliyah just felt so exposed. Before she knew it, tears were falling from her eyes. Eron watched on, each tear tugging at his heart involuntarily.

"Ms. Aaliyah, you can tell somebody roughly sexually assaulted you. You have tears up against your vaginal walls. It's not as bad as it sounds though. You can get dressed. I'll text Eron's phone tomorrow with the results. You can pick up your prescription at the pharmacy." Dr. Angelo walked out the room.

"What prescription is he talking about?"

"We might as well get some work done while we're here. I'ma walk out to the car. Just grab the medicine, and I'll meet you at the car."

So, now I'm a murderer and a drug dealer? she thought.

Aaliyah smirked as she got dressed to head out of the room to the pharmacy. As she passed by, Robin's ratchet ass looked down.

That's your best bet, thought Aaliyah.

Aaliyah entered the waiting room. It was still crowded with dopefiends and young mothers who couldn't control their kids.

"Hi. I'm here to pick up my medicine."

It was then that Aaliyah came face-to-face with the other piece of Eron's foolproof puzzle, Dr. Brown. She immediately took notice that the two doctors were definitely related. Aaliyah smiled, thanking the doctor, and she headed out to the car.

"Thanks," Eron said, grabbing the bag from Aaliyah's hand. Aaliyah noticed that he touched something that made the radio come on and a storage space pop out.

This nigga is heavier than I thought! He serious about this shit huh?

Aaliyah sat there trying her best to look unfazed, but she ended up laughing. "Where do we need to go now, Mitch?"

"Hahaha. Niggas got jokes huh? We should go check on your dad—fuck that—that nigga Calvin to report that he's missing so that you will be eliminated as a suspect."

Aaliyah was silent for the rest of the fifteen-minute ride. The realization of her situation was beginning to weigh heavily on her heart and mind.

"Come on, Aaliyah. Get ya mind right, baby. Matter of fact, this sad shit might work out in our favor."

Aaliyah nodded, hopping out of the truck. Eron walked closely behind her as she approached the door. *Damn! This ass is so fat. How long before those test results come back?* he thought.

It was at that moment that Eron decided that he wanted to get to know her. He wasn't fazed by that murder shit. He participated in shit like that every day. Calvin and his bitch deserved more torture, but death nonetheless. Plus, having a female on his team who could be his shooter would be epic. Niggas weren't expecting shit like that. He didn't have any enemies, but he wasn't sleeping on that. Niggas always want your spot. Eron kept heaters on or around him, and he was licensed too.

Aaliyah immediately walked to her old room. It was clean. Spotless. In fact, the entire house had been cleaned. Eron posted up on the wall as he watched Aaliyah in awe. Her beauty was so simple and breathtaking to him, but he was amazed by how she called the police.

Aaliyah was frantic and crying. "Oh my God! My dad is missing. I haven't seen him in almost a week. He has a girlfriend named Stephanie. Nobody has seen either one. You want me to come file a report? Okay, I can get my friend to bring me. Okay, I'll ask for Detective Morrison. Thank you. I'm sorry for all the crying."

Aaliyah hung up the phone, wiping her face. "Let's go."

Eron smirked as he followed her outside to the truck.

"He said to go to the precinct on Gratiot. I don't think you should go in with me though. What you think?"

"Ummm, shit, I don't know. Maybe I should go in playing the caring friend role."

"Yeah, you're right. That may look better."

Soon, they were pulling up to the Gunston precinct. It was located right at the Gratiot and Gunston intersection. Right across the street was a gas station where many drugs were sold. Bums were even panhandling like it was legal. Aaliyah's face was still puffy, and her eyes were red, so she looked the part of a broken daughter as they walked into the police station.

"Hi. I'm Detective Morrison, can I help you?"

She sniffled. "Hi. I think you're the guy the 911 operator told me to speak with. My name is Aaliyah, and my father has been missing for a week."

"Yes, ma'am, that's me. We can step back into my office and fill out the necessary paperwork." Detective Morrison ushered them into his cramped office. He proceeded to ask all of the procedural questions. It was pretty typical. The Detroit Police Department wouldn't even attempt to find a crackhead. DPD didn't really do their jobs.

"Looks like we have everything we need. Do you have a phone number that you can be reached at?"

"No, I don't have a phone."

"Huh? Who doesn't have a phone in this day and age?"

"Me."

"Well, okay. Well, you can always check back with me. Here's my card. Again, I apologize about your father. Hopefully we'll find him," Detective Morrison said in a tone like he was reciting from a script as he ushered them into the lobby of the precinct. Aaliyah was happy for once that the cops didn't seem to care about Calvin.

Once they made it to the truck, Eron was pissed. "That's exactly why I don't fuck with them shady-ass niggas, dog. What type of bullshit was he on?"

"Man, I don't know. I guess in our case this is a good thing," Aaliyah responded as she reclined in her seat. "Where are we headed to now?"

Eron didn't answer the question. He just stared at her for a couple seconds before pulling off. *What am I gon' do with her? I don't know. But I do know that this is just the beginning.*

Four Years Later

Buzzz. Buzzz.

Aaliyah woke up to the sound of her phone ringing. She didn't even look at the screen. She just answered the call. "What?"

"What you mean what? Get ya evil ass up."

"Eron, what do you want? I'm tired. Where are you at anyway?" Aaliyah said, finally opening her eyes and feeling around the bed.

"Getting to the money. You know where I'm at."

"Okay. So, Eron, whhhaaatt?"

Eron just laughed because he knew that she hated to wake up. "I need you to come to work for a minute."

"That's all you had to say. Where you want me to meet you at?"

"Meet me at Mal house."

Aaliyah didn't say bye, and Eron didn't care as long as she was on the way.

Aaliyah quickly got out of bed. Eron didn't play when it came to getting money. He was a go-getter, and he created a go-getter in Aaliyah. She was him in woman form. He broke bread with Aaliyah. He kept money on her at all times. He taught her that whatever he gave her she should put a portion of toward her advancement. Hell, she was one of the only women who inquired about what was next professionally. It fucked him up.

Aaliyah went to her closet, thinking about what she could throw on. Looking pretty was a must. She noticed that Eron had a Jordan box that was empty.

"The 11s. I think I will do that too," Aaliyah laughed, talking to herself. She knew that Eron would talk so much shit about her trying to match him.

Aaliyah took a quick shower and got dressed. She chose some black jean shorts with a white fitted tank top. She combed her hair down and topped it off with a black Chicago Bulls snapback. Simple was about to go and make some money look.

"Yeah, this'll work," Aaliyah said, looking in the mirror. Eron had made her tone it down a lot. At first, she thought she wasn't feminine enough to wear gym shoes, but Eron brought it out of her. She could wear anything and feel sexy. Eron and Aaliyah had the type of relationship where they were able to talk like best friends, play like kids, argue like husband and wife, and protect each other like brother and sister. They could be lovers and friends all wrapped in one. Eron taught her that any woman could wear heels and have sex appeal, but if you're sexy in simple shit, you just got that "it" factor. Don't get it twisted though. She loved heels, too, just not too often.

"Oh, shit!" Aaliyah said, rushing to her car only to realize that it wasn't there. She looked at keys in her hand only to realize that they were Eron's keys to his truck.

Well, at least he pulled the truck out for me, Aaliyah thought as she hooked up the iPod. She turned T.I.'s *Trouble Man* album on full blast and made the forty-minute ride to Mal's spot.

Ring. Ring. Ring.

"Yes, Eron. I am pulling up."

"Damn, dog, why are you taking all day?" Eron asked quizzically, standing on the porch, watching her pull up at Mal's Detroit home. This was his block. Mal grew up down South, but he had been in Detroit since he was nine years old.

Aaliyah hopped out of the truck, causing Eron to forget why he was mad. *Damn!* Eron thought, watching Aaliyah's thick thighs rub together in her short shorts as she walked into his personal space.

"What are you looking at?" Aaliyah asked, grabbing the brim of his matching Chicago Bulls snapback.

"I see you tried to dress like daddy, huh? My baby is so fucking lame, dog!"

Aaliyah stepped closer to Eron, whispering as if somebody else were there. "My baby shouldn't hit it like he does. He always hit it so well all the time. Sometime I just want to dress like him. I even had his T-shirt on before I left home."

Aaliyah walked around Eron, heading into the house. "Jamal!" Aaliyah bellowed throughout the house.

"Man, get the fuck on with that yelling shit!" Mal answered, coming from the kitchen. They had grown into a real-life brother-sister relationship.

He wore some of the smoothest skin, which was seen on very few men. Needless to say, he was fine. To know him was to love him, unless you fucked with his family or his money. His reputation was not one that would be wise for you to test. He had the soul of a nigga from the South with heart that only one from Detroit can possess.

"Y'all acting mean over here. Come here and give me a hug! Don't act brand new." Aaliyah smirked as she stuck her arms out so that Mal could walk into her church hug.

"Man, you make me want to whoop Eron's ass every day."

Mal always said the same thing. Ever since Eron told Aaliyah how Mal would always help her, she would hug him every time she saw him. The simple act of appreciation low-key let him know just how real Aaliyah was. He thought she was a beauty, not for him but all for Eron. It just took Eron a minute to take notice to the innocent beauty that was tucked away in the hood. Mal had his mind wrapped around a chick named Dior whether or not he truly wanted to admit it. But that was a whole different story.

"All right, Liyah, break that shit up," Eron announced, hating as always.

"Bro, I'm not going to take your girl!" Jamal said, knowing how Eron was about Aaliyah.

"Nigga, you can't take my bitch!"

Aaliyah just shook her head. This was what always happened. They would always bicker about the simplest shit.

"Ugh! Bruh! Did you wake me up to listen to y'all argue? I could still be getting my beauty sleep."

"Yo' ugly ass sure does need all the beauty rest you can get." Jamal frowned up his face.

Aaliyah busted out laughing. "Fuck you, nigga. Yo' mama!"

"I'll be sure to tell her you said that, too."

Eron broke up the session. "Look, I need you to go to Dr. Brown's office. Pick up Sam, Laura, and Rachel. He got scripts for all three. He'll give you what I need."

"Okay. How much am I giving him for all three?"

"Just give Dr. Angelo and Dr. Brown fifteen hundred dollars apiece."

"Why are you giving them so much?"

Before Eron could answer, Mal jumped in. "Aye, sis, it's simple. You take care of who takes care of you. They been looking out, and they don't fuck with nobody but us.

We always got to show our appreciation. You should hear niggas in the street having to find a new doctor to feel their scripts every month. That shit is time-consuming. Time wasted that can be spent making money. They see something in us, so we can't do shit but respect it. Plus, they ain't greedy. The ball is really in their court. Dr. Angelo and Dr. Brown can afford to charge us whatever they want to. They don't do that though. They could go work for the rich people, but they want to help the hood."

Eron chimed in. "That's exactly it. We just humbly looking out for who look out for us. This situation is foolproof. It's a win-win situation."

"Oh, I see. That makes a lot of sense. I was just asking because I noticed that you always give him a different amount every time. Anything else you need me to do, boss?" Aaliyah said seriously. She didn't work for Eron, but she filled in when he needed her to. It wasn't too often, but she was there when he needed her, no questions asked.

In some fashion, she felt indebted to both Eron and Jamal. They never made her feel that way, but her life changed for the better when they came along. They guided and protected her like only loyal, genuine people could do. For that, if it was in her means, she would do the same for them. If it wasn't in her means, then she would rob, steal, and/or kill to make sure they had whatever they needed. They were all the family she had.

Eron squinted. For some reason, he was turned on. It could've been because Aaliyah had no problem asking questions. It could've been that she never passed up the opportunity to learn something. Aaliyah always did that to him at the weirdest times.

"Aye, did you pay our last fee to graduate?" Eron was proud of Aaliyah. In a couple of days, she would be a college graduate. She was a senior in the last days of her last semester at Marygrove College, studying computer information systems. Eron made sure every bill was paid. She wanted to go to school, so he made it happen. Now she was done.

"Yes, sir, daddy sir! All I have to do is show up on Monday!" Aaliyah replied sarcastically. Aaliyah appreciated Eron even giving a fuck because most niggas didn't. It takes a real man to want you to succeed. Hell, it takes a real man to handle a woman with ambition. Aaliyah didn't like how he always had to double-check to make sure she did what she said she would do though. It irritated her, like he was really trying to be her daddy. *Wait! Stop! This is the same nigga who paid for shit to happen.* Aaliyah had to check herself sometimes. She liked to think too damn much, and that wasn't always a good thing. Sometimes it caused her to think up things for no reason at all.

"Hey, I want to ask y'all something seriously," said Aaliyah.

Both Eron and Mal looked up.

"What's next? I really ask y'all to consider how smart you have to be to make some money in this competitive-ass field. But even the smart ones don't make it out all the time."

"It's just a means to an end," said Mal. "My mama was falling short, and she needed me. I had to get out here and get it."

"Much like him, growing up poor makes you want to hustle," said Eron. "Niggas don't come into this with desires to become the next El Chapo, Big Meech, Blade Icewoods, none of the greats."

Aaliyah said, "Hmmm. Well, this was supposed to be a means to an end. Get in and get out. I just think you two are better than what y'all doing. You're meant to be something great. The contribution to society is meant to

be of infinite greatness. I'm just asking y'all to consider
what's next. No, scratch that. Y'all need to pick a goal and
work toward it. You get me?"

"Yeah, no argument from me, Aaliyah," said Mal.

"Aye, Mal, run to the store for me right quick. I'll be
ready to handle that when you get back, bro," said Eron.

Mal chuckled. "Yeah, all right, bro. I'll be back."

Aaliyah smacked her lips. She was confused. She
figured Eron was mad about something she said or did.
He never wanted to argue in front of anybody, including
Jamal. He would either pull Aaliyah away from the
crowd, ask the people to leave, or wait until later. If he
didn't wait then, that meant he was pissed the fuck off.
What the fuck is going on here?

Eron watched as Mal grabbed his keys and headed out
the door.

Eron looked back at Aaliyah sternly. "Get the fuck up
and go in the bathroom! Take that shit off on the way.
You got me fucked up. How you gon' be caring about a
nigga like that?"

Aaliyah looked at Eron like he was crazy. She let out
a sigh of relief. But she was confused. Was he angry
because she gave a fuck about his growth as a man?
He looked almost possessed though. She was stunned.
Aaliyah wasn't sure how to feel. She was kind of scared
yet turned on. Eron had a way of turning her on at the
most bizarre times.

Eron knew that he was taking it too far. He couldn't
help himself though. He had to remember that her
beginnings were rough. Eron never wanted Aaliyah to
feel uncomfortable or unsafe when he was around. He
watched Aaliyah get up, relieving her body of her clothes.
By the time she was on her feet, all she was wearing was a
black lace Victoria's Secret bra, which covered her brown
breasts, and lace "barely there" boy shorts, which her ass
ate up when she started walking toward Eron.

"Damn, girl!" Eron exclaimed. That hard exterior melted seeing Aaliyah in such a state. She was vulnerable to him, and he loved it. He met her halfway. As soon as Eron got up on her, she turned around, attempting to walk away. Eron wrapped her weave around his fingers roughly.

"Where the fuck do you think you are going?" Eron asked, accentuating every word. He began pulling her head back so that it was now lying on his shoulder. He didn't even give her a chance to answer the question before his lips took her lips hostage, like he was trying to suck the money out of them. The passion that Aaliyah felt from Eron's kiss left her speechless. His tongue was fighting hers in a sensual love match.

"Um, um, um, ummm," Aaliyah moaned breathlessly. She couldn't hide the effect that Eron had on her even if she tried. Eron pushed her body off of him, bending her over with one hand and ripping her panties off with other hand.

"Shit!" Aaliyah felt a little piece of her skin rip at her waistline where he tore at her panties. Even that small amount of pain fed into her horny state of mind. Before she knew it, Eron was on his knees behind her, spreading her ass cheeks apart and licking from top to bottom.

"Um. Shit!" Eron began moaning hopelessly into her ass.

Aaliyah's ass was definitely a weak spot for her. She loved it smacked, played with, rubbed, and licked. She was feeling faint. Eron was rubbing her clit and licking her asshole. He began sticking his tongue in and out like it was his dick in Aaliyah's pussy. He kept pulling her ass cheeks apart and letting them go, making them slap him in his face. Eron used his hands to knead and massage her ass.

"Sssss. Oh yeah, daddy, just like that." Eron followed those instructions to the letter. His mouth and fingers switched locations. He latched on to Aaliyah's clit softly yet firmly. Eron sucked her clit in and out of his mouth. He then went to the rest of her pussy, not wanting it to feel neglected. He slid his tongue all around the lips and inner lips that made up her pussy. Aaliyah began rubbing her clit.

Eron jumped back. "Move your fucking hands. I can make my pussy cum."

"I know, baby. I just—"

Before Aaliyah could finish her thought, Eron used his mouth to latch on to her clit, pulling it into his mouth, using his tongue to gently caress her love button. And just like that, he had her cumming in a matter of seconds.

"Shiiittt!" Aaliyah literally felt every single ounce of energy leave her body along with her womanly fluid. Eron felt her body go limp, so he wrapped his arm around her waist in an effort to hold her. He didn't let up on her clit though. He sucked on it like he was drinking from a straw and trying to get the last little bit of juice from the bottom of a cup.

"Okay. Okay. Okay. I can't take it anymore. Please just put it in. I need it."

"What the fuck is 'it'? I don't know what the fuck that is! Tell me exactly what you me to do to you!"

"Shit, Eron, I want you to take that big-ass dick and shove it my pussy!"

"Wait. Whose pussy is it?"

"It's your pussy! It's your pussy. Now please put me out of my misery."

Eron immediately stopped leaning up to push his dick in one quick thrust.

"Shit." Aaliyah was losing her mind. She began throwing the pussy on him relentlessly. She grabbed each ass cheek with her hands. Eron loved to see Aaliyah in this position because her hands were so small and her ass was so fat. He loved the contrast. It was so sexy. Then he had to look at the contrast between Aaliyah's waist and her ass. Eron could wrap both hands around her waist and his hands would touch.

"Damn, baby, just like that." Eron was in a state of euphoria. Once he got behind all of Aaliyah's fat ass, he lost it every time. It never failed. It was now her show. He had to bow out gracefully and let her take the lead in this position. Eron thought her pussy was the best on the planet. Even though he would fuck bitches from time to time, what they had never did amount to the gold that Aaliyah held in between her legs. It was always wet, and it gripped him tight immediately on arrival. He was in love with the fact that he was her only, besides the incident with her bitch-ass daddy. It was loyal pussy. That's what Eron loved the most.

"Ohhh I love this big-ass dick!"

"I know you do!" Eron smirked. He pulled her ass checks apart, making them jiggle and wiggle everywhere. "All this ass. Damn!" He licked his hand, smacking each cheek. He looked up at the sky and starting meeting Aaliyah's shots back. Thrust for thrust. Stroke for stroke. It was a match made in heaven.

"Umm. Eron, you are going to make me cum again."

"That's what daddy wants. I'm always gon' make this pussy cum before I get mines," Eron groaned. He had to put those legs in the air. He pulled out of the pussy unwillingly, turning Aaliyah around and placing her on the couch with her legs to the ceiling. He dived straight in the pussy with Aaliyah's legs pushed back to her shoulders. He yanked her socks off her feet and began sucking and licking on her toes. Eron was never into feet before he met Aaliyah. He loved the fact that she took care of her feet winter, summer, spring, and fall. Now, he wasn't right if Aaliyah's feet were not on him. He needed them to sleep comfortably. Eron didn't even want Aaliyah in the bed with socks on her feet.

Aaliyah started to shake her head left and right, arching her back and moaning Eron's name over and over. "Eron, Eron, Eronnnnn!" Eron would never fully understand what Aaliyah felt when they were intimate. He never disappointed her. He took her to new heights every time. She was always left dizzy with Eron's love. Aaliyah was sure that not everybody was fortunate enough to experience orgasms and love with such a strong force.

That was all it took. Eron pulled his dick out of Aaliyah's wet pussy vise grip.

"Here. Catch it!"

Aaliyah leaned forward with her mouth wide open. She engulfed his dick in her mouth. Eron's dick tickled her tonsils. She began bobbing up and down on his dick recklessly, yet not one tooth touched his dick. Spit and slobber covered his dick.

"Here I cum," Eron growled as he struggled to get the words out of his mouth. Aaliyah started humming a tune against his dick.

"Uh. Uh, shit!" Eron's dick jerked inside of Aaliyah's mouth. "Don't stop," Eron stuttered. He didn't need to say that though because Aaliyah had no intention of stopping until she had every last one of his kids down her throat.

"Oh shit! I'm cumming!"

Eron pulled his dick from her mouth slowly. Once the tip of his dick reached the pout of Aaliyah's lips, she licked them and his dick together, looking at Eron lovingly in the eyes.

Aaliyah walked into the bathroom with Eron close on her tail, kissing the back of her neck.

"Would you go 'head on, man?"

"Shit. I know." Just that fast Eron bounced back into business mode. He grabbed a rag from the linen cabinet, and in the shower, he started to gently wipe Aaliyah's vagina. He made sure it was squeaky clean before he moved on to washing his genitals.

"Aren't you just the sweetest?"

"Dog! Shut up! You know I always gotta make sure 'she's' good!"

Aaliyah busted out laughing.

After they'd gotten out of the shower, Eron said, "I'ma go check on the grow houses," just as Mal came back into the house. On the outskirts of Detroit, Eron and Jamal each had a grow house. A grow house is a place that is used for nothing but to grow and package marijuana. Both houses held sixty-two plants apiece at any given time. They were going to follow their young bulls A.J. and Ro to the house to break down the weed and distribute to the dealers.

In one of their meetings with Dr. Angelo and Dr. Brown, Eron and Jamal were introduced to Jomo. Jomo was a thirty-two-year-old straight from the island of Jamaica. He was looking for a low-key way to get some USA money. Jomo knew exactly what it took to make Kush. It was potent, and it was what the streets wanted. He wasn't looking to sell small time. The smallest he wanted to sell were ounces, pounds, and bows. Jomo was very close friends with Dr. Angelo, so naturally, he went to his friend with his problem. In turn, Dr. Angelo set up a meeting to see how everybody could benefit from the situation.

"Nigga, you ready? You know we can't be late," Mal said.

"Yeah, bro. I know. We should be good on time though. I just gotta make sure Liyah straight. You know I hate having her going to work and shit. This shit ain't for her. We need to keep her record squeaky clean so she can do her computer shit."

"I know, bro. You can always have Jessica bum ass do it. Bitch ain't got shit to lose."

Jessica? What the fuck do they need her for? "Why she got to do it?" Aaliyah immediately snapped.

"Shit, girl can get on the bus. I ain't putting you on no mutherfucking Greyhound."

"Aye, sis. It's just business." Jamal was always the voice of reason.

"You know what? You right. Fuck it, it's all for the sake of the almighty dollar." Aaliyah shifted her eyes from Jamal to Eron. "You better hope she knows her place. I need you to understand that I will leave."

Eron squinted. Just the thought of Aaliyah thinking of leaving had him feeling a certain way. She provided him with something he didn't know he was missing. Aaliyah was Eron's equal. She was him wrapped in womanly curves with a heart attached. Aaliyah was a thinker, whereas Eron operated off of impulse. It could be bad if each had to stand alone, but together they were unstoppable. You fucked over Eron, and he was on his way to come gunning for your ass. Aaliyah would try to calm him down to think of a plan. She saved him from catching plenty of cases from acting on strictly emotions.

"Man, the bitch is just going to work, that's it."

Aaliyah smirked, sliding her tongue across the front of her teeth. "For your sake, that's all it better be." Aaliyah turned away from Eron, walking over to Jamal to give him a hug.

"Be safe," Jamal warned.

"Y'all too," Aaliyah replied, walking off.

Eron just shook his head at Aaliyah's stubbornness. "Bye to you too."

"Bye."

"Man, make sure you go straight home when you get done," Aaliyah heard Eron say as she hopped into his truck. She watched as Jamal and Eron hopped into the car and pulled off in the opposite direction. Everybody had their own agenda, yet they were all headed to do the same thing. That thing was work.

"Wait, Ms. Aaliyah, I'ma stop you right there. I think this is a bit too much. Maybe even a little past my pay-grade," the therapist said with an exasperated sigh. She handed me a business card.

"Excuse me?" I said. "You get me in here acting like you care. Or like you want to help me. But you shut me down because my story is too intense?"

"That's not what I'm saying. Not at all. All I'm saying is this is out of my paygrade. You should go downstairs to the victim support group. Have a good day." She sat back at her desk, lifting her hand in the direction of the same door I'd come in.

Have you ever been so mad that your skin just starts to get hot? That's how I felt. I wanted to call her every name in the book, but I wasn't into begging or trying to convince anybody that I needed them. Even if I did.

"I know you're upset with the way things are going, but if you don't take anything else away from this session, take this: sign up for the victim support group."

"Yeah, yeah, now you care?" I snapped, grabbing my coat and my bags and rushing out of that therapist's office. I was so frustrated that tears welled up in my eyes. I angrily wiped them away. Something pulled me down the steps toward the location of that victims' group.

My mind was everywhere else as I attempted to pull the door open, only to be yanked toward the door. But somebody pushed as I was pulling, causing us both to smash into the door and drop the things that were in our hands.

"What the hell?"

"Oh shit."

We got ourselves together. Nobody apologized. We made eye contact. Both of us had tears in our eyes.

"Well," I said, "since you not trying to apologize, can you please point me in the direction of a"—I looked at the business card in my hand—"Dr. Jennifer Long?"

She smirked. "I guess I could." She pointed into the room.

I winked. She walked away.

Chapter Four

Tineya

"Hey, Dro. What's up?"

"What you mean what's up? Where you at?"

"I had an appointment earlier." I shivered, thinking about my therapy session. "Now I'm leaving the shop. Salena paid for my hair appointment today."

"That's what's up. I got a minute. I'm trying to see you."

"You got a minute huh? That's all I'm worth huh? Even on my birthday huh?"

"Oh shit." Dro smacked his lips and blew a deep breath. "Man, ain't nobody forget your birthday. That's what I was calling you about."

"That's what you were calling about? Yet we been on the phone with no 'Happy birthday' in sight."

"Man, look. I ain't playing. I got something for you."

"Yeah, okay. Let's go grab some lunch."

"Okay, yeah. We can go get some carry-out and go back to your place."

"No! I want to go out and sit down to eat. You know what? Never mind." I hung up my phone. Feelings of becoming irate started to take over my body. *You know what? Fuck him.*

I turned the car radio up, making my way to my apartment.

"Man!" I said, pulling into the carport at my apartment. I took my time getting out of the car. I watched as Dro walked up to the building, waiting for me as if he were invited.

He said, "Don't be rolling your eyes. I just wanted to talk to you."

"So talk, Dro!"

"Damn, it's like that?"

I walked in, flipping my asymmetrical bob and unlocking the door.

"Man, here."

I took notice of the bag in his hand for the first time. It was a silver and black Kay Jewelers bag. Grabbing at it, I noticed it was light in weight. *Jewelry is light, duh!*

"That's some money to help furnish ya spot," Dro said. I pulled out three tight coils of money. This nigga put some money in a gift bag. I couldn't lie. The apartment was scarcely decorated. It needed some love. But I'd just recently moved in, so it was in the works. Call me dumb, but I expected something with a tad more meaning. Nonetheless, I was appreciative.

"I guess this is the type of gift the side chick gets huh? No paper trail, right?" I smirked. "Thank you." Yeah, I was giving him a hard time.

"Dog, really? You serious?" Dro smacked his lips.

"I said thanks. Appreciate it."

"That shit don't even sound sincere."

"Did you get me a card?"

"Damn, nah. I forgot."

"Hmm." I nodded, with my lips tightly pressed together, corners pointing toward the ground. See, he said he forgot the card, but I knew better. Dro knew cards were important to me, but he stopped that years ago. Yeah, he a thorough hood nigga, but I was sure that the nigga forgot my birthday. I was tired of the nigga. "It's cool."

"Nah, it ain't. I fucked up."

Peeking into the bag again, I couldn't help the frown that graced my face. For some strange reason, I felt the need to call my uncle. And I didn't want to do that in front of Dro. I went inside my apartment. Dro followed me, but I went into the bedroom and closed the door. I called my uncle.

"What up?" he said.

"What's up, Unc?"

"Nothing, nothing, chilling with this little therapist I know."

"Oh okay. You been too busy."

"I really don't got time for this shit. You get money in your account religiously, so I don't know why you bitching."

"Huh?" I was lost as to why Uncle Nathan was treating me like I was scum on the bottom of his shoe.

"You heard what I said. What did you need?"

"Look I just needed to vent."

"Not surprised."

"Dro is here. He bought me a gift for my birthday. The gift was presented nicely. It was in a Kay Jewelers bag. But in the bag was no jewelry, no card in sight. Do you think I have a right to be mad?"

"No, you do not have the right to be mad. At least he got you something. Side bitches don't get gifts. I think you should close your mouth and be happy you got somebody. Especially considering your handicap. Most niggas don't want to deal with that."

"You know what crawled up your ass. But fuck you."

"Fuck me? I'm all yo' fucked-face ass got. And you need to stop going to that therapy shit. It ain't working."

Nathan hung up the phone, leaving me flabbergasted. I was so confused. We'd never had anything remotely close to an argument, so this was eating at me.

After my parents died, I moved in with my uncle Nathan. After the death of my parents, I always felt that I was left with mental scars as well as the physical ones. The feminine part of me hated the way I looked. I felt as though I could hide the mental scars, but the long scar on my face always brought questions, stares, even jokes.

Knock, knock. "Can I come in?"

"Yeah," I grumbled. "Welp, that was thoughtful."

"What you mean?" he asked, fingering my newly done hair.

I knew what he was doing. I slid away from his touch. "Stop! Nice bag. Who just puts money in a bag for somebody he supposedly cares about?"

"What kind of woman don't like money? And what you mean stop? Now I can't touch you?" He continued to move my hair, making it cover my eye as much as possible.

"Stop. Damn."

Just watching him move and look so stupid made me think about how we met. Dro and I met in such a bright light, I could barely fathom how things went so dark. How so much time had passed but no growth had happened was mind-boggling. The nigga Deardo, known to the hood as Dro, had been around since my very first day of high school. Dro was my first everything. Hell, he was my only thus far. Yeah, I was grown ass with only one sex partner. But anyway, it'd been years and many different bitches. I knew the nigga's parents. He even had a consistent girlfriend he'd had for about two years now. Why was I even entertaining him? I hated change. I mean, shit, I hated even going to new schools.

As well as I knew Salena, I was sure her ass probably already expressed her feelings about Deardo, also known as Dro. Deardo, ugh. I should've kept it pushing once I learned his real name. But anyway, she had all the reasons in the world to not deal with that nigga at all. For as long as I'd known her, Salena had always had a protective nature. If she wore her feelings on her sleeve, she wore her hate for Dro on her forehead with braille letters so that even a blind man couldn't miss it. Yup, her hate for him ran that deep. But when somebody you were rooting for lets you down, that shit hurts.

But anyway, let me take you back to the day I met fine-ass Dro. Don't judge me. He was fine. I just disliked the fact that he was a simple-minded, ol' "I give a fuck what people think" nigga. Woosah.

It was the first day of my ninth-grade year at Denby High School. I'd just met a girl named Salena the same day, and she was cool. All of the students were made to meet in the auditorium to pick up their class schedules. I was so nervous about meeting new people. The pressure wasn't that strong because I at least had Salena with me. While I was new to the school and area, Salena wasn't. She knew enough people from the hood.

"I'm mad as hell that we gotta wear these weak-ass uniforms. It's almost like they want us all to look the same. How this shit gon' start as soon as we finally get to high school?" Salena was pissed.

"I'm happy about it. I don't need nothing else to bring any more attention to me. I just want to blend in," I admitted, tugging on my uniform shirt and trying to stretch it over my booty.

"You kill me saying that shit. You were born to be different. If God wanted you to be the same, then He would've made us twins. You pretty even with that shit on your face. You see these bitches?" Salena pointed to an ugly girl walking by, causing me to chuckle. I still finger combed my deep swoop, making sure at least a portion of my scar was covered. At least then it wouldn't seem as bad. Well, at least that's the rationale that I came up with in my head.

"Damn, she got a fat ass."

There were different groups of students standing around and trying to get into the auditorium. That statement caused me to wonder two things: who had said that and who were they talking about?

All the people who were around looked up, trying to be nosey.

I still to this day asked God why I even looked up. Maybe if I would've ignored it, then shit wouldn't have gotten hectic. Once I turned around, that's when shit just went left.

"Ugh. Damn, what the fuck is that on her face though? All that ass with that ugly-ass scar on her face."

I swear I was stuck. Me and this boy actually caught eyes. That was all the confirmation I needed to know that he was talking about me. My feelings were all over the place. I couldn't stop the tears even if I tried. It was almost as if a floodgate opened up, releasing an ocean that was my tears. In my head, I was slapping the shit out of this nigga. I was lost as to why he was fucking with me. My back was to the nigga, so he couldn't say I was staring at him or anything.

"Bitch, you got me fucked up!" Salena snapped me from my shock. I quickly reached out, grabbing her shirt and pulling her toward me. Shit, if anybody was going to check this nigga, then it would be me. I had some emotional scars, true. I had a lot of shit going on, but I wasn't soft by a long shot. What would I look like having Salena swing first? I was cool if she swung second, though.

"What y'all bitches gon' do? How the fuck you mad 'cause that shit on yo' face got some shit on its face?"

When this nigga said that, a small crowd erupted in laughter while others looked at me with pity. To say I was embarrassed would be an understatement.

Something in me snapped. I mean I knew I couldn't take this stocky-ass nigga out. But I wanted to. I didn't even have time to call my uncle. I thought back to something my daddy taught me about fighting before he died: "If you feel scared, there is no such thing as fighting fair. Fuck it, there is no such thing as fighting fair period. Play to win, baby! It's either you or them. You ain't no boxer, so you don't have any rules to abide by."

I put my head down as if I were just walking by the unnamed boy. Once I was close enough, I balled up my fist, hitting him dead in the center of his nose. This precision hit caused his nose to start leaking instantly. How did I know to hit him there? Shit, I was from the hood. I heard that's where you aim. Honestly, that was pure luck. I figured no matter if I got my ass beaten or not, I hit his ass.

"Dog. What the fuck?" *the dude yelled while he stood there in shock for a couple of seconds. I was sure he expected me to maybe talk a little shit but not to actually hit him.*

"Oh shit." *Salena snapped me out of my daze. I started backing up. It was at that moment that I knew I fucked up.*

"Nah, bitch, you ain't getting off that easy!" *Next thing I knew Salena was pulling me away, but something wasn't right because I felt an even bigger, stronger, more forceful pull. That pull landed both me and Salena on the floor, confused as fuck.*

"Nigga, you about to really try to fight some females?"

This deep voice came from deep in the center of the sea of people. I could've sworn I saw the light, a hand reaching to me from the heavens.

Sike. LOL. Let me find out y'all ain't never seen *The Wood*. But nah, anyway.

I heard a deep voice yell out to the boy, stopping him from pummeling me.

"Fuck this ugly-ass bitch! Dro, this ain't got shit to do with you. This bitch hit me!"

"Nigga, you think I'm about to continue to let you talk slick to some females? You always on this fuck shit, arguing with females and shit. And I'm damn sure not about to let you hit her."

Salena and I both looked at each other, shrugging our shoulders as if we were asking each other if either one of us knew him. We both came up short with the boy's identity. I took note that both dudes were wearing football jerseys with their uniform pants.

"Fuck all that." This nigga reached around Dro, trying to tag my dumb ass. I ducked just as this Dro person picked the dude up as if he were picking up his toddler pushing him. Salena grabbed my stunned ass, pushing me to the back of the crowd.

The dude gathered his footing, pushing Dro back.

"Steph, nigga, we cool. This ain't what you want though, dog. Go ahead on, man."

"Fuck you, nigga. This ain't your fight. Yo, dog, you see my eye? That bitch got my shit leaking. She won't walk away from this shit!"

I watched from the back as this nigga was scanning the crowd for me. His eyes went back to Dro, taking a swing.

I hope this nigga does not get his ass whooped trying to save my ass.

If I felt like shit before, I would feel like a fucking manure plant if Dro lost trying to fight my battles. Hell, he might've wanted to beat my ass. All because of this fucking scar. The root of all my problems. This scar.

"Damn, he fucking that Steph dude up!" Salena snatched at my arm while putting her balled-up fist to her mouth. She leaned back, blowing into her fist.

I looked up in time to see this Dro dude serve up a two piece and biscuit. The only thing missing was the man on Mortal Kombat *saying, "Finish him." No exaggeration, the dude Steph dropped to the ground. He was laid out on the ground, snoring. I'd always heard about somebody being put to sleep, but I'd never known it to be true.*

"Damn. Man, let's make this a half day and get the fuck out of here." I shrugged as I quickly grabbed up Salena just as the student officials and the Detroit Police Department's gang squad started to flood the school's auditorium. I learned early on at Denby when the gang squad showed up that somebody was going to jail. Calling Unc to come get me from jail? Ha! Not on my to-do list, especially after him taking me in. He was barely old enough to be my brother. So, no, no, I would not be adding to an already overflowing bill. Not to mention my uncle wasn't the type who wanted to visit a jail in any shape or form.

"I guess we walking home from school today then, huh?" Salena asked, giggling.

"Yeah, I guess so."

Salena and I started to make the short trek home.

"So, have you talked to Shawn?" The second the question left my mouth I began to regret it. Shawn was Salena's brother, my uncle's friend. Shortly after I came to live with Nathan, Shawn was slapped with a couple years' sentence. He was charged with intent to distribute. Shawn and Salena were as close as a brother and sister could be. Needless to say, I probably shouldn't have brought up the subject.

"Yeah, man, I talked to him today before school. One day at a time. Today he's closer to coming home than he was yesterday, right?"

"Right!"

I loved that about Salena. She was tough. Even if she was hurting, nobody was going see it unless she wanted you to.

Just like that, that was the end of that discussion. Salena said nothing else. And if you knew Salena, then you knew if she didn't want to talk, you should just leave it alone.

Of course, the walk home got quiet until a horn beeped, causing us both to roll our eyes. Horn blowing is for whores. Mama taught me that early on. So we kept walking. I turned around at the sound of a car door opening. In Detroit? I looked at Salena, giving her the eye. We were about to take off like some track stars.

"Whoa! That's how y'all do the nigga who's catching notches on his belt for y'all? I mean I'm still seventy-two and zero." The guy Dro approached us, jogging.

It wasn't until that moment that I was able to get a good look at him. Damn, he was fine. He had brown skin, and he was tall and commanding with dark eyes. That was enough for me, man. Nah, he wasn't pretty by anybody's definition. He had a rugged look about him. Well, as a rugged as a high school student could look anyway. Unconsciously I took about two steps behind Salena, pulling my hair down and covering my scar as much as I could. Placing something over my scar had become a habit of mine.

"Thanks for what you did back there." I couldn't help but speak up. I mean the incident was my entire fault. As much as I didn't want to talk, I had to thank the boy.

"Yeah, that was real stand up of you. Appreciate it," Salena finished, sensing I was uncomfortable.

"Thank ya kindly. You're far too kind," Dro came back, laughing at himself and quoting Jay-Z. He shifted his eyes to me. I felt it. I didn't meet his stare though. I mean why would I? Looking in his eyes meant that I would see

the same questioning look that I hated. While I was left smitten, he would pity me. He would have a questioning look. I was out of my league, and I knew it.

"What's y'all names?"

"Salena."

"Scar."

Salena rolled her eyes, smacking her lips. I knew she wanted to say something, but she didn't.

"Scar huh?"

I nodded.

"Call me sometime, Scar."

"Yo, Tineya, bring it back." Dro waving his hand in my face brought me back from my wicked-ass daydream.

"Stop, dummy!" I smacked his hand from my face.

"Look, I know I been messing up, but I appreciate you sticking around. I need you to rock with me. I can make it up to you."

"How so?" Don't judge me!

"Man, what you doing for your birthday?"

"I might go out."

I watched Dro's whole demeanor straighten up as if he was aggravated.

"What you gotta go out for? I mean shit, we can stay in, chill, and watch movies or something."

"I know, but I'm tired of letting this day get the best of me. And I said I *might* go out."

"I mean shit, fuck that going-out shit. That shit over-rated. I like that you my chill girl. You don't have to do all that extra shit." Dro basically put an end to the conversation.

One thing about this nigga was I knew him. He was genuinely a sweet guy. I mean we were friends before we leveled up. Nah, I couldn't even say we leveled up because it sure didn't feel that way. I'll say since we started to fuck around. Like literally nothing changed but the date on the calendar and my ability to see through his charades.

See, he wanted me to himself. Yet, he wouldn't commit to just me. See, Deardo and Salena were really my only friends. They were who knew my story. Both knew all my demons and battles in dealing with my parents along with my battle wounds and scars. There was a big difference between Dro and Salena though. Salena would never try to keep me in or play into my weaknesses. She was always uplifting from the time I officially met her.

Dro was the exact opposite. Once we started having sex, it was like he wanted me, but he wanted me in the dark. He was my first. Sex with him always got better and better. If I wasn't sure about his feelings for me, they always poured out during sex. Sex was never an issue. After we crossed over from "just friends" to "more than friends," he would say little things. He would say enough but think he wasn't hurting my feelings. You know the whole "you cute, but you have that scar." "You got some grade A pussy, but you have that scar." "Your body is out cold, but you have that scar." "I love you, but you have that scar." "I want you to be my girl for real, but you got that scar."

How was I supposed to get over this scar while it was being thrown in my face disguised as a compliment? Who else would want me with this scar? Was it just easier to deal with somebody I'd been dealing with forever? For so long I'd been dealing with this, but I could honestly say I was tired.

Dro started walking in my direction. I quickly stood up, pretending to stretch. I just didn't want him to get me on the bed.

He stopped midstep. "Damn," slipped from his mouth.

I looked down at my clothes, realizing that I only wore the famous Instagram outfit: gray sports bra and matching gray boy shorts. See, Dro was crazy about my body. Always had been.

He took his hand, using only his index finger to rub up the curve of my waistline.

"Nope. Deardo. G'on 'head on. Ain't shit up."

"What you mean?" His voice dropped on octave or two. This was something that only happened when he was horny. He pulled me into him, talking into my neck.

Don't judge me. Just that fast, I was all in, but he didn't have to know that. I could use the distraction.

"Nah, I'm straight. It's already been taken care of," I whispered.

Dro's body stiffened. He quickly recovered as if something flashed across his mind. He continued kissing my neck and rubbing all over my body. "You ain't crazy, baby. You know a nigga would lose it if somebody else touched what's mine."

He yanked my shorts down while pushing me back onto the bed, with his two fingers resembling a gun with his eye over his thumb. It looked like he was looking through a scope. The fool even had one eye squinted and leaning into his makeshift gun. He pulled his makeshift hammer back on his makeshift gun.

Crazy-ass nigga, right? Okay, no judgment, but that crazy-ass shit turned me on. I'ma tell y'all why. When you love a nigga, but you know a nigga don't love you how he should, this is the only point of our "situationship" that I knew the nigga loved. His mean, evil ass was soft in the bed. He gave it all to me. But only in the bedroom. It was the only time I felt all the love.

"But let me check to be sure." He took a long, deep smell, damn near putting his nose up in my pussy.

"Um."

"Nah, this my pussy." Using his tongue, he took a long, soft stroke from the bottom to the top of my pussy.

"Wait." I couldn't take it, so I slid back on the bed, planting my feet on the bed for assistance.

"Nah, ain't no running." Dro hooked his hands around my calf muscles. He mimicked the dogs on the "feed the animals" commercials, looking so uncomfortable.

"Um. Um. Ummmm." I was fighting a losing battle. When the nigga got his hands on me, my body just reacted.

Slurp. Slurp. Lick. Lick.

"Dro."

"Yum. Yum. Yum." He was in a zone. His mouth was sopping wet, almost mimicking somebody using a biscuit to wipe up the gravy. He pulled and pushed my clit in between his lips with a good amount of pressure.

"Shit, I'm about to cum."

"Good!" Dro ran his face all around the lips around my pussy. He was allowing my juices to flow all over his chin and lips.

Dro lifted his body up, coming eye level with me. He placed soft kisses onto my sensitive skin. I was putty in his hands.

When did we get to the bed? I breathed deep, my chest going up and down.

"Open up, Tineya." He used his knees to open my legs wider. He rubbed his thick mushroom tip up against the opening of my pussy. He used it to coat his dick and spread it all around my vagina.

"You gon' let me in?" He asked his rhetorical question not waiting for an answer. He inched his way in.

"Hmm."

"Sss."

The first contact was always intense, always as if he were breaking through walls. No pun intended.

"Girl, you think I don't love this shit? Damn."

"Shut up." I shook my head feverishly. I didn't want to hear that shit. I was mad at him. I was hurt by him. I hated that I loved him. It always amazed me. A person could make you feel amazing in one situation, yet that same person could make you feel the lowest. So, you see, I didn't want all that soft shit. I wanted to fuck. I didn't want to hear Dro sell me dreams. At this moment, I wasn't buying.

"Nigga, who you talking to?" he questioned with a knowing smirk. "What you want to do?

"Shit," was the only answer I could get out as he continued to open me up.

"Huh?" He went in. In and out. Out and In.

"Let me get on top." I continued to push up toward him.

"Yeah? You got that."

He flipped over, pulling me with him. I took my time to adjust to his dick. I began to rock slowly. Up, down. All around. Up, halfway down. Pelvis-to-pelvis grinding.

"Damn, girl!"

That was all the ammo I needed. I went from being down on my shins to planting both feet onto the bed. I was placing my forearms on my thighs, causing us both to go crazy. Our grunts and moans took over the room.

"Umm."

"Uh. Uh. Uh."

Somehow Dro sat up, wrapping his arms around me, and began to trust his pelvis into mine. I matched him, meeting him halfway.

"Wait, where'd you go?"

"Stop. I want it from the back. You know I can't be doing all that for a long time."

We laughed together as we repositioned.

I felt a long lick from the front of my pussy to my asshole. I shivered. Dro then licked the chunkiest part of my ass cheek.

Smack!

"Ouch! Stupid!"

"Shut up. Damn. Anybody ever told you that yo' ass talk too much?"

Giving me no time to even think about his smart-ass mouth, he plunged into me deep and forceful. I could only gasp.

"I don't see yo' ass talking no more."

Challenged accepted.

I threw my breasts into the bed, making the arch in my back deeper. I went to work. I concentrated on the task at hand. I crashed my hips into him. Fast. Then slow. Working my hips in circles.

"Whoa. Shit! Slow down."

I knew I had him right where I wanted him. I slowed up. I clenched my walls around his dick.

"Girl. Come on. Stop fucking playing. I'm about to cum."

"Uhhh!"

"Where you want me to put it?"

Knowing just what he liked, I used my hand, pulling my ass cheeks apart. He liked the contrast of my little hand on my juicy ass.

"Here it cum."

Splat.

We lay flat on the bed, me on my stomach with Dro lying on his back.

"So, I was thinking maybe after I handle a little business we can go to dinner or something."

I looked up with a blank look as he came from the bathroom. As strong as my poker face was, I was jumping for joy on the inside. I wanted to hang out with him.

"All right, Tineya. I'll be back here to get you in about three hours."

Ring. Ring. Ring.

"Nothing more irritating than this iPhone ringtone," I

said, waking up. "Damn what time is it?" I wondered, turning on the light and sitting up in my bed. I started to hear heels clicking down the hallway, coming toward my bedroom. My phone was ringing at the same time.

"Damn. Okay. You look nice! You looking like the best money that I've ever spent," Salena said surprisingly. "I mean besides the fact that you look like you just woke up."

I couldn't help but laugh at Salena's ability to have a full conversation with herself.

"Where you was going? Or coming from?" she questioned, sitting in the chair in the corner of the room. Things hit me like a ton of bricks. "You better not cry! Just tell me what's wrong."

"Dro."

"Hmm. What a surprise. What happened?"

"Man. He weak as fuck. I don't know why I allow him to do this shit to me. He pissed me off. I asked him to come eat with me after I got my hair done. He gave me every excuse in the world why he couldn't come to lunch. He ended up on my doorstep with a Kay Jewelers bag."

"What, Tineya?" a surprised Salena asked.

I put my finger up, signaling her it wasn't like that. "I look in the bag. A Kay Jewelers bag, expecting jewelry. You know, nothing too meaningful but a piece of jewelry. You know, since it's a jewelry bag."

"Tineya!" She was over me extra in my explaining of the bag.

"It was money in the bottom of the bag."

"This nigga Dro is stupid."

"Yes, girl, he gave me some money to furnish my spot. How romantic. Now don't get me wrong, I'm appreciative of anything anybody gives me, but I'm looking for some kind of validation of what we're doing."

"I get it. His stupid ass should've done more. Hell, he could've gone lighter on the pockets and gotten something more meaningful."

"My sentiments exactly. But here's the kicker: we go back and forth for a while and end up having sex. Of course he all in his feelings. Letting emotions and shit come out. Even said he wanted to hang out after he handled some business."

"Damn, Tineya. Don't tell me this nigga stood you up."

"Sure looks that way. That was hours ago. I don't even have a missed call, no text. Not even a fucking smoke signal." I could only chuckle to keep from crying.

"Aye, don't you drop another fucking tear on Dro's sorry ass. Today is your birthday. I don't care if it's damn near over. Go freshen up, and we'll go to that party that Nathan was talking about."

"I don't really feel—"

"It wasn't a question. Come on."

I got up with a smack of my lips.

"And, Tineya, even though Dro is a big disappointment, it's not my decision to make. I won't even attempt to offer an opinion tonight. I just want you to enjoy tonight and worry about tomorrow tomorrow."

"You got it."

Big Sean and Metro Boomin's "Savage Time" blasted through the club's speakers as we made our way inside. The club was way too crowded by my standards, but I was keeping that comment to myself.

"Aye, y'all beautiful ladies need a booth?"

A promotor walked up to us immediately, trying to get us to pay a couple hundred for a booth. Since there were probably a million different niggas on the bill, the promotors would attack you just to make a couple dollars.

"Yeah, I guess so, since it's my baby's birthday."

"Hmm. Straight up? Oh, I guess I gotta look out for the birthday girl."

"Look who's already got a booth. Sir, I appreciate it, but my uncle's already here. Thanks anyway."

The promoter just turned around without a response.

"Somebody's mad."

"And nobody gives a fuck," Salena said with a shrug as we made our way toward Uncle Nathan's table. Uncle Nathan's eyes damn near popped out of his head. Salena grabbed at my arm, pulling me back into her chest.

"I know he's an asshole, but he's your uncle. He was wrong to talk to you like that, but he loves you."

How did Salena know about the words me and Uncle Nathan had? Hmmmm. One thing I picked up along the way was to never show the right hand what the left hand was doing. Some underhanded, sneaky shit was going on, and I knew it.

"Yo, my muthafucking people in the building. Happy birthday, niece!" He grabbed Salena and me, hugging us roughly. He was way past his limit. This nigga!

"Hey, Unc."

"Hey, Nathan."

Uncle Nathan leaned over to his two homeboys, and they stood up, escorting the women they had out of the booth.

"Now y'all will have a little bit of room. What y'all drinking?"

That's why I fucked yo' bitch, you fat motherfucker.

The club went crazy just off hearing the beginning of one of the most classic diss records ever, no disrespect to any of the greats or the late greats.

"Ayeeeeee!" We turnt all the way up. For a minute, I relaxed. It felt good. But hearing Tupac made me think about my father. It wasn't a bad feeling, but it was a feeling nonetheless.

I tapped both Uncle Nathan and Salena. "Hey, I'm about to run to the bathroom."

"Aye, Salena, go with her for me."

"Of course."

"No, y'all go ahead." I gestured, flicking my wrist. "I'll be right back."

"Okay." Salena put up her hand, turning up her cup. "Text me if you need to."

"I'm straaaigghht!" I copied a Tip lyric that very few would know, causing Salena to call me a lame.

I was really not feeling the snake-like movements that were going on with the people around me. After what seemed like a million "excuse me's" later, I finally made it to the restroom. *No line. Thank you.*

I walked in, running right into a mirror. I was shocked at what my reflection showed. For the first time, I was pleased with what I was looking at. Originally, I put on a dress, heels, and the whole nine for the date that never happened, but then I wanted to go for a more comfortable set of clothes.

Very few knew that I loved clothes. I'd wear anything from cheap to high-end clothing. I would find anything from Walmart or resale shops. Tonight I wore a tight, deep V-cut bodysuit in addition to the amazing Victoria's Secret bra that had my 34-D's looking much bigger than they really were. Nobody really knew that my titties were not as big as they seemed, and it didn't matter that the girl who measured me at store was hyping me up. I was choosing to ride this 34-D wave.

Don't judge me.

The high-waist jeans accentuated my midriff, which was smaller than my ass. Not that help was needed in that area. I wasn't sure if it was the liquor, but I was appreciating what I saw for once. My evaluation of myself caused me to look up. I stood making eye contact with myself, which was something I'd hated doing since my birthday in 2007.

The bob hairstyle was a signature look of mine. Since I wasn't into long hair or the way it looked on me, the "framed face" look worked. The left side part allowed for me to cover most of my forehead, thus covering as much of my scar as possible. Simply because of the way it allowed me to cover most of my face, it was all I wore. The makeup was minimal for a number of reasons. I didn't believe in false advertisement. I couldn't present myself one way and mislead somebody. Besides, while I could appreciate the ability to enhance myself, I just wasn't into the caked-up look.

"Shit. Let me go to the bathroom before niggas come looking for me."

The second the stall door was shut, I heard a rush of girls come in all loud and belligerent.

"Now let me see this bracelet D crazy ass bought you."

I proceeded to handle my business in an attempt to get out of the bathroom.

"Girl. Yes. I found the Kay Jewelers bag in his car. He was so mad, saying that I blew the surprise." The girl laughed a drunk laugh. I just knew that the bitch's tongue was hanging out. Ugh.

What the fuck?

I knew that this wasn't a fluke. This was Brandy, Dro's girlfriend. Or not his girlfriend. Either way, they were involved. She'd been around for a while.

"OMG, it's a charm bracelet! What does the charms mean?"

"Girl, I don't know. I don't care. It a nice piece though. The way it shines. Yesss!"

As I stood there hearing the main door of the bathroom slam, I was more curious than ever, as if a light clicked in my head. Bitches love social media. I pulled out my phone, searching to see if maybe she posted a closeup of the bracelet. Not even five minutes later, I was zooming in on a very vivid picture of the bracelet.

The caption read, "When bae not your bae but you still get surprised like you bae. Side note: Don't go snooping because you might ruin the surprise." Then there was a winking emoji.

I came out of the bathroom stall, shaking my head. Reason three million why I shouldn't have a word to say to Dro's ass.

Swallowing the lump, I was done crying over this nigga. As soon as I opened the door to walk out of the bathroom, not only was Salena on her way in, but the deep scowl on her face made me stop in my steps. I looked dead in the eyes none other than a drunk, surprised Dro.

Another fucked-up thing to remember about my birthday!

Chapter Five

Aaliyah

"Baby, wake up."

I heard what Eron said in my ear repeatedly. I just chose to ignore him. I could feel his body weight leaning over me. He knew I was not a morning person, not even for his fine ass.

"Aaliyah, get yo' ass up."

"No!" I snapped with one eye open.

Eron's stupid ass covered his mouth and nose with one hand. "Dog, I should beat yo' ass for talking to me with that foul-ass morning breath! Fuck wrong with you?"

"Nigga, fuck you." I laughed, jumping up from the bed.

"You know I don't give a fuck how bad your breath stinks. Bring your ass here." He grabbed my face, giving me the most nasty and stinking-ass kiss.

"Uhhhhh! Get the fuck off me. You may not care, but I do. You know I hate that morning breath shit." It was true. I hated morning kisses. I strongly felt that you should handle that before being all in someone else's face.

"Ohhhh, shut up. Anyway, I gotta go to work. I just wanted to make sure you were up to go make it to that new counselor."

"To work? Nigga, bye." I took off, locking myself in the bathroom. Eron hadn't punched a clock since I'd known him. However, he operated like a man on a mission. There was no sleeping in. Even if he stayed in the house, he was making some type of moves from there. I wanted him working in something lucrative and fulfilling to him.

"Are you going to work today?" Eron questioned.

"I'm not sure if I'm going to just not go today or if I will just go in for a half day." After years of sitting out because of the accident, I started working as an assistant in the IT department. I'd worked my way up from an IT assistant to the IT administrator with an assistant of my own. The company was understanding of my need to move around. Sometimes sitting was not a good thing, but neither was walking or standing. Because of intensity of the accident, I had pain and nerve damage in my legs that would probably never go away.

"I love yo' childish ass. Don't allow how that other therapist made you feel to make you miss out on your elevation. This shit is not about her. I want you to be the best you can be."

I couldn't stop the blush that covered my face if I wanted to. This might have been a real mushy moment if the shower weren't running while I sat on the toilet. "Okay."

"I'm serious."

"Okay, daddy, damn."

"And don't be overworking yourself. That 'Jake from State Farm' nigga assistant of yours can hold shit down for a minute."

I busted out laughing.

"I don't know what yo' ass laughing at. You know his ass look like he sell insurance. Dog, khakis be so pressed. Tell his ass that nobody wear the creases down the middle no more. His polo should be tucked in but pulled out just a tad. Grandpa-ass nigga."

I was dying with laughter as I stepped into the shower. "Oh my God, stop. Don't you have somewhere to be?"

"Yeah, I'm leaving." Laughter was very evident in his tone of voice. "And quit it with that daddy shit before I come in there and fuck you. And you know ain't no flimsy-ass lock gon' stop me."

"That's enough about me. I just needed to introduce myself for the newcomer. Her name is Aaliyah Banks. She had a not-so-good experience with a colleague of mine, so she's come to join us."

I stood awkwardly as we all took each other in. I couldn't help but notice the pretty girl I kept seeing around. She seemed shy and mad awkward. I was taken aback by the scar on her face. It just made me wonder what happened. I didn't think the scar was bad at all. Shit, it made the woman look like strength.

I looked at the woman I now knew as Dr. Jennifer Long. She was a nice-looking Puerto Rican woman. The world would probably pronounce her as a plus-size woman because of her huge breasts and the small pouch that hung over the black dress slacks she wore. It was evident that her behind was huge, as it hung off the sides of the chair. While her body wasn't the best, her face was something out of the magazines. Her face was beat to perfection. Her hair was honey blond and long. Like, damn near to her waist. Her eyes were piercing.

I didn't like the vibe she was giving off though. She didn't seem real. I wasn't sure what it was. I wasn't sure if I trusted her. Her true feelings would reveal themselves. They always did.

"Ohhh, what happened?" Not able to see exactly who asked the question, I just answered.

"Man, she was extra siddity. She allowed me to open up with some of my story but then didn't let me to finish. I believe she used the phrase 'not in my paygrade.'"

"Uh! No, she didn't."

"Go ahead, Aaliyah, have a seat. See, that's part of the reason people don't like to open up. But I digress. I hope that doesn't alter what you want to share with us."

"Umm, a little bit."

"Well, I'll say this. I want each and every person to live their best version of their lives. Please don't allow a person who is living their life hinder you from living yours."

I felt that. I couldn't allow this woman to stop my progress and growth. Ether one of the therapists. I had already declared to Eron, and more importantly to myself, that I would give this therapy thing my all. Hell, trusting the process didn't mean I had to trust either of the therapists personally.

"Uhh!"

Everybody's heads snapped in the direction of a man slouching down in his chair. He wore a black Lacoste collared shirt. The shirt was paired with black jeans. Black high-top Air Force Ones were on his feet.

"You got something you want to say, Aaron?" Jennifer asked with a surprised look on her face.

"Man, this polished-ass girl? What the fuck is she doing in this section with us mutants of the world?"

"Is this nigga serious? Mutant?" I asked, looking around the room and settling on the Tineya girl, who just shook her head.

"You know what a mutant means, right? A freak of nature. Something that will cause people on the street to stop and stare. You know how innocent kids will point to you, asking their parents why you look like that?"

"I know you calling not only yourself but a roomful of other people mutants is stupid. How can you educate people on being different when you're playing into their ignorance about people who are different?"

"She is absolutely right. What makes you think that you belong here and she doesn't?"

He chuckled in a really manly way, leaning to place his elbows on his knees. He snatched his dark sunglasses from his face with a yank. "This is what makes me need to be here."

His eye was dangerously lazy. In addition, his eye looked as if he might've been caught in some type of fire. I didn't budge though. Grabbing the chair and sitting down, I was preparing to snap on this nigga.

"I'm going to intercept right here. This is a group with a strong vision. This is a group of strong values. We want to offer support and resources to those seeking to heal themselves. This victim support group is just that: a group of people who need support. Regardless of what anyone thinks, if you're in here, then you're here for a reason. Even me. We are all seeking to live positive, healthy lives. And just because you don't see the scars doesn't mean they aren't there. I want Aaliyah to tell us why she's here, and we'll go from there."

"Okay. It's a pretty long story."

"Start from anywhere you want to. I think that's a good spot to start. And I do mean anywhere. That's what we do here. We tell our stories, and we compare, contrast, and vent about them."

The memories just began to flood my mind. It's crazy, because I remembered everything, from the intricate details to the minor.

Chapter Six

Aaliyah

"See, it was me, Eron, his homeboy Mal, Dior, Ashley, and Sincere. Eron is my man. I'd met Dior at my school. Ashley is her cousin, who lives in Atlanta. Sincere is her boyfriend. See, it only feels right to tell the whole story. I mean, in telling my story, I may have to get into a little bit of my family's story."

"Go ahead."

"Do tell."

"The same patient-therapist confidentiality applies, correct?"

"Correct," Dr. Jennifer Long replied with a chuckle. "There are even laws that protect a patient from another patient, like in a group setting."

"Duly noted."

I began to hear all types of affirmations from the small group, and even the ignorant dude began to loosen up. Slightly.

Eron and Jamal had been rocking with each other since they were little shorties. Eron, his mother Ms. Tina, and his father Big E lived on Detroit's east side on Lakeview when Jamal and his mom moved next door. Jackie, Jamal's mother, was a single parent, but you would never be able to tell because she made sure that Jamal was a man's man.

It was a summer day when Ms. Tina stood on the porch talking to Big E and Eron when the moving truck pulled in the driveway of the house next door.

"Finally. I was sick of that house being vacant," Tina said to her husband.

"Yeah, me too."

Ms. Tina was a bold woman, and as soon as the lady and her son stepped off the truck, she went over to introduce herself. "Hi. Welcome to the neighborhood."

"Ohhh, I didn't know we get our own welcome committee on the east side. I hear this is the bad part of the city," Jackie said jokingly.

Ms. Tina immediately liked the lady. She also couldn't help but notice her thick Southern accent.

"Hi. I'm Jackie. This is my son, Jamal."

The ladies shook hands as Tina called Big E and Eron over to them. "This is my husband, Big E, and our son, Eron."

"What up, doe?" Big E said with a nod, and Eron followed suit with the same greeting.

"What it do?" Jamal greeted Big E. He felt his mother looking at him. "Sir," he added as he chuckled.

"Wha' you laughin' at, li'l woe?" Jamal extended his hand, noticing that Eron was laughing. Jamal was not completing his words like most people from the South would do. "Sup? What's funny, bruh?"

"That country accent!" Eron laughed really hard as he shook Jamal's hand. Jamal laughed with him.

"Y'all just propa up here," Jamal said, chopping off the "er" from the word "proper."

"All right. Good to meet y'all good people, but we got a ton of work to do."

Big E looked at the big U-Haul truck. "Is somebody coming to help y'all?" There was no way that Big E would let them move all of their furniture by themselves.

"Yeah, but we'll manage. Hell, we packed and loaded the truck by ourselves. We should be fine."

Big E looked at her like she was crazy with a second head sprouting from her neck. Big E was a lot of things, including a gentleman. "Eron, come on. Let's go change clothes."

Eron headed toward the house with no questions asked. When Big E spoke, your best bet was to just listen. His dad was a nice guy when it came to women. Tina even had to realize that Big E wasn't flirting all the time. He just believed that a woman shouldn't have to stress. Big E made sure Tina lived well and never had to do "hard work."

"Wait. Big E," Jackie yelled after him, but Tina interrupted her.

"You can stop. That's the kind of man I married. No woman will work hard around him. Your best bet is to just listen. Welcome to the neighborhood." Tina walked into her house to get changed.

Jackie looked at Jamal, puzzled. Jamal smirked and immediately held so much respect for a man he met less than five minutes ago. That was realest shit he ever witnessed.

"I might like staying here after all."

Chapter Seven

Aaliyah

Jamal and Eron cruised on the freeway to meet Jomo. Two of their young bulls were set to meet them at Eron's grow house, and then they were to headed to Jamal's.

"Aye, man, you remember when yo' contra ass came up here sounding like the nigga in *Snow on tha Bluff?*" Eron quizzed, teasing Mal.

"Man, fuck you. Get yo' 'They-call-me-Lil-P-I-represent-the-CP3' nigga."

The nigga really dropped a line from Lil Romeo's song "My Baby." He was moving his hand and head like he was spitting a hot sixteen.

"Oh shit, nigga, you got me about crash!"

They both were full of laughter. Eron couldn't stop laughing.

"Anyway, nigga. Damn, man, today gon' be long as fuck, bro," Jamal said, breaking the laughter.

"Man, I know. Who do you got meeting us here again?"

"That nigga A.J., and Ro is going to come out here too."

Eron smacked his lips. He couldn't stand that nigga A.J. He was the loud type who liked to look and act like he was running shit.

"I know, but the nigga does his thang with that weed shit. Plus, he doesn't mind taking road trips. We kind of need dude," Jamal declared, leaving a sour taste in his mouth.

"Bro, I know you ain't just say that we need that nigga! Nah, you ain't say no fuck shit like that. What the fuck? We found that nigga, so we'll find another one."

Jamal just shook his head as they sat in front of the house. "Would you stop fucking yelling at me, nigga? Now you know that is not how I meant it. Right now we got this nigga where we want him. We are going to have to let this nigga hang himself." It wasn't that Jamal liked A.J. He just tolerated him. Jamal figured it was smart to play a nigga like A.J. close.

Niggas like A.J. were not permanent fixtures in this game. He just worked for the moment. At this point, Jamal felt that it was best to keep their enemies close. He knew just like Eron knew that A.J. liked to play big-boy games, but he was a bottom feeder. Mal and Eron were on a realistic level. No, they weren't in the game to be millionaires. They wanted to mine the game for all they could with all wins and no losses. A.J., on the other hand, didn't have the qualities that it took for a person to lead. He was the type who saw the gold at the end of the rainbow but didn't want to take the necessary steps to get it. Like when people saw somebody living their best life on Instagram, but didn't see what it took for them to get to the money. You didn't see the blood, sweat, and tears that were put in. He was that guy. He wanted the aftermath of hustling.

"Yeah, all right. Let's get this over with," Eron said angrily as they hopped out of the car.

As the duo made their way on the porch, Jomo came out and greeted them in his white lab coat. He was serious about this shit. "What up, doe boys?" Jomo's accent was still strong as ever.

Eron and Mal laughed. They always did when Jomo tried to sound like a Detroiter.

"Fuck ya fuckin' bumbaclots!" Jomo smirked. "Come on so I can show you fucks what's ready to be distributed." Jomo led them into Eron's grow house. The house looked really homey. It even looked lived in. Eron and Jamal watched as Jomo put the code into the keypad to the steel door. The three of them were the only ones with the code. Eron changed the code as often as every week so that he would know exactly who was in the house.

The basement was huge. Jomo had the magic touch. He was a chemist. He knew what to add to make the Kush what the streets wanted. In Detroit everybody smoked weed. The Kush man usually smoked weed. Kids smoked weed. Mothers smoked weed with their kids. Nobody wanted bamma-ass weed though. Reggies was a no-no. They paid top dollar for good, grade A Kush. That's what Jomo was able to whip up.

"See, this side of the room over here is ready for distribution. I know y'all don't care to hear the technical part, so I won't go there. I'll have to come back probably in two weeks to check on the development of the rest of the marijuana. And if you look over here, I started some plants to replace the bunch that's being bagged up today."

"Okay cool," Eron said. He understood the weed-growing process was a tedious process. This is why they didn't care to learn to grow the weed themselves. Jamal thought it would be smart for both him and Eron to get their weed cards. This put them at an advantage, because if they were ever stopped by the police and by chance had some weed on them, then they had papers for it. They vowed to never have more than the allowed amount on the card on them. You had to be smart about this street shit.

Knock. Knock.

Eron turned around, pushing the code to let A.J. and Ro in the room.

"Ol' security-guard-ass nigga!" Jamal joked.

"So what, nigga? We can't afford to lose in this game. Rather be safe than sorry. We ain't even hittin' no real money for real."

Jamal opened up the door and immediately knew that Eron was going to be pissed when he saw the fuck shit A.J. was wearing.

"What up, Mal?" Ro said, shaking his head knowingly.

"Dog, what the fuck you got on?" Eron asked A.J.

"What you mean? You always are fucking with me, dog. Why though?"

"'Cause you always looking like a ol' Rico-ass, Nicky Barnes–ass nigga. All I'ma say is nobody bet' not run up in my shit, because you got arrows, pointers, and signs over your mutherfucking head saying drug dealer! Don't come back to work dressed like a clown. Ol' Ronald McDonald–ass nigga. Come on, Ro, let's get this shit done."

Eron's rant left A.J. looking dumb just as it always did.

"All right, Jomo, thanks as always."

"All right, bruh!"

Eron and Ro headed toward the basement. "Oh, my bad! See ya, bro. Hit me up."

"Fasho, bro. I'ma lock up. Jomo, you can just follow me around there since you ain't got to stay too long."

Chapter Eight

"Look like we done, boss man," Ro announced as he weighed and wrapped up his last pound of weed.

"Bro, don't hit me with that 'boss man' shit!" Eron laughed. No matter what Eron said, Ro always called him boss man.

"Dog, you are the boss to me. Well, you and Jamal are the boss, collectively. I understand that in order for a nigga to be a chief he got to be an Indian first."

Eron couldn't do shit but accept that shit. Real niggas understood that there was a process when it came to leadership. Ro knew that it was best to let somebody lay the blueprint and use that as a guide.

"Ro, you are definitely one of the real ones. That shit is going to take you far."

"Fa real! All right, boss man. I'll text you once I make it to put this shit up."

"All right, be safe." Eron pulled off, tired as fuck. He turned on some of T.I.'s *Urban Legend* album and made his way across town to his home.

Eron sighed. He didn't feel like arguing with Aaliyah. *Let me call her ass and test the waters.* "What up, doe?"

"What up?" Aaliyah greeted Eron, rolling her eyes.

"What are you doing still up?"

"Nothing."

Yup, she still mad! "Yeah, all right, dog. I'll be there."

"When will you be here?"

"When I get there. That's when I'll be there," Eron snapped, throwing his phone in the cup holder as he came off the freeway heading toward Jessica's house.

Eron stuck his key in the door. Jessica lay on the couch in a robe, looking at him. Jessica was surprised. "Girl must've made you mad, huh?"

"Dog, shut the fuck up. All you do is run ya dick sucker. Come put this in your mouth," Eron demanded, unzipping his pants.

Jessica just opened her mouth wide. This was all it took for him to get her, very minimal talking. Eron didn't even have to step out of his Mike's. Jessica went to work. She would have him out in fifteen minutes.

"Uh. Uh. Uh, shit!"

Jessica swallowed all his seeds. Eron wiped his dick off. He immediately felt like shit. *Why the fuck did I do this dumb shit?*

Eron put his dick up, walking out the door.

"So you just are going to leave like that? That's how you are going to do me?"

Eron never answered. He never even acknowledged that Jessica said anything.

Eron drove up his street, thinking about the war that was awaiting his arrival. He took his time getting out of the car. He took a deep breath before sticking his key in the door.

Man, I don't feel like this shit.

Eron exhaled, opening the door. The sight before him was the sexiest shit he'd ever seen. He stood in the doorway, taken aback by the sight before his eyes. Aaliyah stood at the stove with her back to him. She wore a white beater and bright pink boy shorts. He was confused because most of her ass was exposed. Aaliyah abruptly turned around with a plate in each of her hands. She made T-bone steaks, smothered potatoes, and corn.

It was way too late to be eating, but her man came in late, and she wanted to make sure she fed him even though he pissed her off. He felt worse than he ever felt.

Oh, well it's over. She won't find out.

Eron didn't even realize that he was hungry until his stomach growled. His nostrils finally paid attention to the aroma.

"Are you going to stand there staring all day or eat?"

Eron chuckled, "I think I'm going to do both." The couple sat and ate in a comfortable silence until both of their plates were cleaned.

"Damn, baby, that was good as fuck."

"Thanks."

Eron knew from her tone that shit wasn't sweet. But he didn't feel like getting into that shit tonight. Eron just wanted to shower, fuck his bitch, and sleep comfortably.

"Come on, let's go to bed," Eron demanded, grabbing Aaliyah's hand and leading her to their master bedroom. It was definitely his favorite part of the whole house.

Aaliyah was a weirdo. She had a thing for gray. The walls showed that with dark gray paint with a lighter shade of gray pinstripes. On the far wall sat their California king–sized bed with a wooden headboard and footboard. The centers of both the footboard and headboard were made of soft cloth with different shades of gray. In front of the bed sat a black leather couch with gray accent pillows. On the wall in front of the couch was where a seventy-inch Vizio smart TV rested.

Aaliyah went straight for the bed where she lay watching Eron relieve himself of his clothes.

"Did you already take your shower?"

"Yeah. Well nah, I took a bath."

Eron didn't say anything else as he headed in the direction of the master bathroom. The master bathroom held double sinks, a Jacuzzi tub, and a separate space for the toilet and shower. Eron stepped into the shower and turned on the overhead. He loved the way the water beat against his body, washing away the filth of the day. Eron lived a hectic, busy lifestyle. Sometimes the shower was the only peace of mind he was able to get. Eron used the shower to wash away the stress of the day. He stepped out of the shower, drying off and dropping the towel as he headed straight to the bed.

Aaliyah lay in the bed on top of the covers with socks on her feet. Eron mean mugged Aaliyah as he stood over her in the bed.

"What are you staring at me like that for?" Aaliyah wondered with her face all balled up.

Eron didn't answer the question. He just walked to the part of the bed where her feet lay and snatched the socks off her feet.

Aaliyah giggled. "You are a fucking creep!"

"You need to stop wearing socks in my mutherfucking bed."

"I wear whatever I want to in my bed."

Eron took each foot in each hand, and he began rubbing them, going all the way up to the soft spot on her hip that she liked so much.

"Ssss."

He followed the touch on her hip with light, wet kisses as he pulled her panties to the side. Aaliyah held some of the best pussy he ever tasted. It always smelled fresh, and the way Aaliyah's pussy leaked when she was wet was always making his mouth water. He took his tongue, and in one long stroke, he licked from the bottom to the top of her pussy.

"Uhhhh." Eron felt Aaliyah's body shudder. Eron loved that, regardless of how angry Aaliyah was with him, her body always betrayed her, giving in to him. That was the type of shit that made his dick even harder.

Eron went in for the kill. He put Aaliyah out of her misery when he latched on to her juicy clit. He softly began to circle her clit, making sure that his mouth was pouring with spit. Aaliyah told him a long time ago that the wetter the mouth, the better the head. No woman wanted a stiff-ass dry tongue. That was how he ended the night. If Aaliyah was pleased, then he felt that his job was complete. Eron lay at Aaliyah's waist, and they both slept like babies.

"Wait. Pause," the girl Tineya asked unbelievably. "So you knew about him cheating?"

"Not initially. No, I didn't. The girl told me of course. Then his ass came clean. If you want to call it that. We 'broke up' for a short while. In that time we became friends, and honesty came with that. The nigga was brutally honest. He exposed me to a lot of shit that he probably shouldn't have. We sort of began confiding in each other."

"Ohhh. Okay. Makes sense."

"Okay, go ahead. Finish. This is getting good," a seemingly quiet girl said.

Everybody laughed. It made me laugh and feel confident in telling my story. I continued.

Aaliyah woke up the next morning in an exceptional mood. She glanced around their room and ended the gaze on Eron. Aaliyah knew that they were not living the best, but they were not living the worst either. Eron was far from perfect, but he was definitely worth the headache. Aaliyah was a hood chick, coming from one the roughest parts of the city, yet she was graduating from college the next day. At the present moment, she just felt so blessed. Aaliyah had to say a prayer as she pulled Eron closer.

"Dear God, I come to you as humbly as I know how. I just want to say thank you for everything that you do and don't do for me, for us. I pray that you continue to give us the strength to know that we are not fighting our battles and demons alone. I pray for the safety of Eron, Jamal, and myself. Amen."

Aaliyah looked at Eron. He was still knocked out. She was actually surprised that he was still in bed. Aaliyah began to tickle Eron's neck and place kisses all over his face.

"Dog! Get that fucking dragon breath the fuck away from me!" Eron said, full of laughter.

"Ohhh, fuck you! Get up! We have to get the graduate ready!"

"Awww shit nah. My bitch is graduating tomorrow!"

Aaliyah went crazy with giggles. "Fuck you! I'm going to get in the shower."

"I'm coming too!" Together Eron and Aaliyah took a quick shower. Just as they were getting out of the shower, Eron's phone was ringing.

"What up, bro? Everything go smooth?" Eron asked, referring to the packaging at his grow house.

"Yeah, bro, shit went real well. But what y'all got up though?"

Eron thought for a second. "Shit, I don't know." He looked at Aaliyah. "Aye, where are we going?"

"The first stop will be the mall."

"We are going to Somerset. I guess she is going to use this graduation as an excuse to spend my money."

Jamal chuckled, "All right, bro, in a minute."

Aaliyah was already dressed in her colorful summer dress with silver Gucci sandals. She accessorized the outfit using silver diamond studs and a diamond cross. Eron finally had the chance to begin to get dressed.

I don't feel like putting on no clothes.

Eron slipped on a T-shirt and basketball shorts, and he stepped into some cool gray elevens. "You ready?"

"Yeah."

The duo headed to the truck to make the trip to the Somerset mall. The Somerset mall was located on the outskirts of the city. It was a huge mall with a huge escalator in the middle connecting two sides. The side that held Macy's was what black people considered "the poor side," and the side that held the Gucci and Louie stores was considered "the rich side."

Eron and Aaliyah pulled into the Saks Fifth Avenue entrance since it was always easier to find somewhere to park.

"Oh, I was about to say call Mal, but I see his car."

"He got here quick. Well, ain't no telling where he was at though."

Aaliyah and Eron walked into the mall right at the men's shoe department. They could shop apart, but they both liked the way the other one dressed. Eron already liked fashion, but Aaliyah heightened the addiction. Don't get it twisted though. He wasn't with European-cut jeans at all. If the jeans had skinny anything in the name, he wouldn't do them. He was a hood nigga to the core and labels would never change that. Eron loved that Aaliyah could and would rock anything from cheap to expensive. Labels didn't make her. She made the labels. Aaliyah picked up some red Aldani Bally high-top sneakers.

"Damn, Liyah! These muthafuckas cold as fuck."

"Sir, did you need to see a size?"

"Yes, sir, you're right on time. Can I have these in a 12D?"

The man hurried to the back to check for Eron's size while they sat and discussed what Aaliyah would wear.

"I think I want to do your color. I can make my shoes my pop color. Shit, I don't know."

The man brought the shoes out to Eron. "Did you need to try them on?"

"No, sir, you can just ring them up."

The salesman rang them up, and they preceded to the women's shoe department. Aaliyah immediately spotted some multicolor peep-toe Yves Saint Laurent heels. Eron made the purchase, and they were on their way out into the mall.

"So what it feel like? I mean you're about to be a college graduate," Eron said as they walked through, smiling. He was really proud of her accomplishing a goal that she set for herself.

Aaliyah smiled. "I don't think it's really set in just yet. I'll probably cry tomorrow though. People's entire family will be there supporting them. I don't have a single relative who fucks with me. Hell, I don't even have friends. My only two friends are my boyfriend and his best friend. I mean, I ain't tripping off no bitches, but shit, it would be nice to have a female perspective. I operate and move just like a nigga, 'cause that's all I had was niggas teaching me."

By this time Eron was in full-blown laughter. "Dog, shut the fuck up. You are not a nigga, and you don't act like one. Fuck yo' family. They're the ones missing out. You got a hell of a support system in me, my mama, Mal, his mama, and even Big E from behind thick-ass prison walls and barbed-wire fences. Aye, blood doesn't make you family, but loyalty does. Don't forget that shit. Now you about to graduate in less than twenty-four hours, and you acting like a bitch."

Aaliyah popped him upside his head as they were walking into the Louis Vuitton store.

Chapter Nine

The sight before them stopped them in their tracks. Jamal was in the store with a female paying for her purchase. Eron wasted no time.

"Well, well, my brother, what do we have here?"

Jamal looked up with not a surprised look but a "here we go, let's get this over with" look. The girl turned to look at the man carrying the deep voice.

Aaliyah was shocked when she saw who Jamal was with. Her name was Dior. She'd actually seen her on Marygrove's campus.

"Hey, Ms. Lady, how are you?" Aaliyah questioned.

Dior smirked because she knew exactly who Aaliyah was. They would stop and chitchat around the school, but they never really kicked it. Aaliyah noticed that the bitch was fly, and Dior noticed the same thing. They had a mutual respect for each other's presence and style.

"What up, doe? How have you been? I haven't seen you around much."

"I just been waiting on graduation to come and go."

"Yeah, I know. I can't wait until this shit is over."

"So, I got to ask. How do you know my brother?" Aaliyah asked, watching Eron and Jamal chop it up and make purchases.

Dior blushed. "That's a different story for a different day, but I'll definitely tell you. Plus we would have to sit down and talk about it."

"Ohhh cool, we can just grab a bite to eat."

Dior fell into full-blown laughter. She always knew there was something cool about Aaliyah. Most women hated on other women, but it was all love, and they didn't even really know each other.

"All right then, we can all go to J. Alexander's since it's here in the mall. I'm all done getting last-minute shit for graduation. Are you done?"

"I just want to go into Herve Leger to grab this baby doll dress, and then I'll be done." Aaliyah wasn't too worried about getting a new bag. She could always come back. She really wanted to know how Jamal and Dior knew each other.

Aaliyah had Eron and Jamal grab a table while they made a quick trip to grab the dress. And quick it was. Aaliyah called Eron as they made it into the restaurant.

Eron answered, "We are on the left to the back." Aaliyah disconnected the call as she and Dior made their way around the restaurant. Aaliyah paid close attention to Jamal as he watched Dior come toward the table. The look that his face held was that of uncertainty and desire.

The girls slid in next to their dates. Dior immediately introduced herself to Eron. After her rendezvous with Jamal, she kind of researched him and found out that Eron was his best friend and the man in the streets. Actually, both of their reputations spoke volumes around the underground streets of Detroit. They were now tackling legit businesses. Yup, Dior had done her research.

"Hi, how you doing? I'm Dior."

"What up, Dior? It's good to meet you. Good to finally put a face to a name." Eron smirked, causing Dior and Jamal to do so too. Aaliyah looked on, a little baffled by the exchange.

"What the fuck? Y'all know something I don't know?" Aaliyah wondered aloud, looking at Eron and Jamal.

"Man, I just heard about li'l mama. That's your bro."

"Um. Okay."

Dior held the group in suspense. They had idle chitchat throughout dinner. Aaliyah and Dior talked about school, finding out that they had quite a bit in common. They both went to Mike from Salon DNA to get their hair styled. Not only that, but they both had early hair appointments tomorrow morning before graduation.

Aaliyah couldn't take it anymore. "Okay nah, shit. How do you two know each other?"

"Damn, Liyah, you nosey as fuck. It was like this—"

Jamal was interrupted by Dior. "I think I should tell it. It's my truth, and I don't give a fuck if they accept it. No disrespect, but you'll probably want to judge."

Eron spoke up. "Man, this is your story. Who the fuck are we to judge? Shit ain't all sweet this way."

Jamal and Aaliyah nodded in agreement. Jamal felt good that his brother was coming from a positive place.

"Okay, here it is."

Chapter Ten

Dior's Story

"Your remaining balance for your tuition will be five thousand dollar," the lady in Marygrove College's business office said smugly.

Dior just smirked because she was used to females throwing her shade. She smiled at the lady as she counted out the five stacks from a ten-stack bundle.

"Here you go!" Dior responded, watching the ugly broad's eyes grow to the size of saucers. The lady had the nerve to look mad as she handed Dior her receipt. Dior grabbed her receipt and proceeded down the hall with her mean walk in Christian Louboutin's, clicking down the hall.

Dior was a head turner in every sense. She had this aura about her that you would notice before you noticed her beauty. She put most in the mind of Tika Sumpter, Malik's girlfriend from the show *The Game,* and her body mimicked the rapper Nicki Minaj. She had milk chocolate skin, pretty light brown eyes, and gorgeous full lips. She didn't have the biggest breasts, but they were perky and more than enough in most men's eyes. Now, her ass was a different story. It was full, plump, and soft. Her waist was so small that her ass looked like a mountain sprouting out. Her body would've put some of these models to shame. She was authentic in every sense of the word from her body to attitude.

She continued to her car as her phone started ringing.

I got my change up; they looking like they surprised.
Niggas hatin' on me hard cause my paper right

Dior couldn't do nothing but bob her head and down to the Wiz Khalifa ringtone, because that was the story of her life. She checked the time. 6:00 p.m.

"Hello."

"What up, baby? I'm trying to see you like ASAP! I got my homeboy with me, too," replied A.J., this sexy, getting-money-ass east-side nigga. At least that's what he appeared to be. A.J was six foot three and weighed 220 pounds. He had brown skin and was fine as hell. He was a little extra, but his money was long. Well, long enough to trick it off.

All Dior could do was shudder because she got to have her two favorite things: money and two niggas in the bed with her. She didn't do it often, but she liked that shit. Dior was different. She was an expensive bitch who loved to have two dicks in her at the same time, one in her pussy and one in her mouth. The sensation she received was that of another planet. It was like each thing complemented the other. Her pussy would get extremely wet and her mouth even wetter. It was all in the technique. If she was getting fucked right then, there was no limit to how many times she could cum. Although she really enjoyed it, she was very selective about who actually got it. She fucked niggas. They didn't fuck her. It was her fantasy, so anybody she picked would drop funds for it.

"Baby, you already know money is the motive!" she retorted. It was her usual comment when any nigga called her asking for a "favor." Fair exchange ain't robbery. So, Dior wasn't tripping. She couldn't give a fuck about how people viewed her.

"Come on now, baby, you insulting me! Don't I always look out handsomely?" A.J. answered arrogantly.

"That's very true!" Dior knew he respected her hustle, which was why she dealt with him. "When and where?"

"Now, I got to go out of town by nine. I'm at MGM, room 1210," A.J. told her as he hung up. Dior didn't care that he hung up on her because his dick was good, but the money was always better. She never gave a price because he always left no less than $2,000.

Dior proceeded quickly in her smoke gray 2010 Audi A8 to the Lodge freeway toward MGM. Dior was not regular. She exceeded expectations, especially once people found out how she liked to get down. She was a freak, simply put. She did shit in the bedroom that most bitches would like to do but were too embarrassed to speak it into existence. She looked at sex as something that was just supposed to get better every time. She felt each nut should be better than the last. If not, then what was the point of fucking?

After the fifteen-minute ride, she called A.J. as she was pulling up to MGM's valet.

"What's up, baby?" A.J. answered.

"I'm pulling up. What's the room number again?" Dior replied.

"1210," A.J. replied.

As Dior stepped out of the car and headed toward her trunk, the sound of bass caused her to look back. She noticed a black 760. The car was slick, but that wasn't what she liked the most. The driver stepped his Louis Vuitton's on the pavement and was damn near gorgeous. His dark chocolate skin looked somebody whipped it by hand. He wore a full beard and not too big but perfectly pink plump lips. Dior noticed all of this from the corner of her eye as she pretended to search for her bag, which was clearly visible in her empty trunk. She grabbed the bag, closed the trunk, and began to turn around, only to notice that the guy was standing over her shoulder.

"What's up, pretty lady? I'm Jamal." The Southern accent allowed Dior to know that he was not from Detroit.

Dior stepped back, looking him up and down. "Look, I'ma be honest. Your little sneakers are cute, but I don't fuck with the help," Dior stated, strutting off inside the hotel. She picked up her phone and dialed A.J. Glancing back, she saw that the young boy was smirking at her. What Dior didn't know was that he embraced challenges. He never wanted a woman who was easy to get.

Dior proceeded to the elevator and pressed twelve, taking her to the floor she need to be on. The room was right by the elevator, so she made a quick left and knocked. The door swung open, causing A.J. to appear with his deep-dimple smile in a wife beater and sagging True Religion jeans.

A.J.'s eyes looked Dior over from top to bottom as she stood in the doorway. *Her swag is mean,* A.J. thought, pulling Dior in for a hug.

"What's up, baby?" A.J. greeted Dior.

"Hey, daddy," Dior returned affectionately.

They were so caught up in their embrace they never heard the elevator doors open.

"Ahem." They heard someone clearing his throat.

Dior turned around first. *Damn, is this crazy-ass nigga following me?* Since A.J.'s face was in her neck, he didn't see that it was a guy walking their way. *He is so fucking fine.* Dior's mind was going crazy within a five-second period. A.J. finally looked up, but what he did when he looked up was what blew Dior's mind.

"What up, boy?" A.J. said as he and Mal shook hands.

"What's up, A.J.?" Mal returned the greeting. He was staring at Dior from the corner of his eye. Dior used that opportunity to walk in the room. As most men did, they followed her as her big ass swayed from left to right.

"Damn, my bad. Mal, this is Dior." As A.J. made introductions, Dior's thoughts were everywhere. *I hope this
nigga don't say he tried to get on.* Dior didn't know why
but she didn't want A.J. to know her business.

"What up, baby? How you?" Mal said with a smooth
Southern drawl that was beginning to turn Dior on.

"Hey, I'm good!" Dior replied smugly as she began making her way to the bathroom. She felt their eyes all over
her when she began to walk. The room was really spa-
cious. She noticed that A.J. sat on one side of the room and
Mal was on the other. Dior had been in the hotel plenty of
times but never in this particular suite. She felt eyes on her.
As she was crossing the bathroom threshold, she looked
back, and sure enough, Mal was all in. She gave him a wink
while he gave a smirk.

"Damn, she bad as hell!" Mal was still in awe about the
beauty who had just stepped in the bathroom.

"I know she bad as fuck. Been fucking with her for a
minute now. Ain't never met a bitch like her! She about
her money, and I respect that if I don't respect nothing
else. She a freak, too, man."

"She about her paper huh?" Mal was amazed that
she was the one they were about to get down with. He
expected somebody of a lower caliber, not someone as
bad as Dior. Her aura had him in awe.

"Hell yeah, the bitch is fly, and she always solo," A.J.
replied.

"Damn, so she just gets down like that?" Mal asked. He
just didn't quite understand it. *She ain't no bum bitch. I
know she riding good,* he thought as he glanced down at
bright red bottoms that she kicked off before going to the
restroom.

Of course, Dior was listening as she freshened up. She
was not offended. Now, if there were no money on the
floor, this type of situation wouldn't be up for discussion.

"Oh, shit, nigga, fuck all that when you get there. Make sure the shit is quick, man. Don't fuck with none of them bitches. Just get in and get out. No fuckups! She gon' meet you here in a minute," Mal told A.J. as he handed him a bag he was carrying when he walked in.

"Man, I got you," A.J. replied kind of quietly because he really didn't want Dior to know that he wasn't the one calling the shots. She and everybody else thought he was running shit, but he was just a mule. Mal and Eron paid him well while he played the back seat, or at least that's what people thought. A.J. was more of the flashy type like Rico from *Paid in Full,* while Mal and Eron were more like Ace mixed with a bit of Mitch.

Straight up? Stunting-ass nigga! Dior was fuming. She hated niggas who played roles. *Fuck it. He always break bread with me!* Dior's thoughts continued to run rampant.

Dior decided to bless them with her presence. She came out of the bathroom in a brown Victoria's Secret panty and bra set. Dior stood there for a few seconds and let them take everything in. She never gave any eye contact to either guy.

She looked at A.J., and he looked to be in a trance. His eyes had a glazed-over look. She looked at Mal and noticed that his face was straight, but his black True Religion jeans were doing very little to restrict his dick.

A.J. was a pussy eater, so by the time Dior looked back at him, he was pulling her to the bed. He took her panties off in one rip, diving head first in the pussy.

"Shit!" That was all Dior could manage to get out of her mouth. A.J. licked her from top to bottom slowly with so much expertise. He pulled her pussy lips back, licking each layer.

"Umm. Yeah!" Dior was in a state of euphoria. She didn't even notice that her eyes were closed until she opened them and Mal was looking her straight in her eyes. She looked down and saw his dick jumping, causing her to lick her lips. He took the hint, taking his jeans and drawers off in one stroke. His dick was much larger than Dior thought. Her mouth got so wet. Dior looked down. A.J. was making his way to her clit. The anticipation was driving her mad, causing her to squirm.

"Ummm!" Dior let out an exaggerated moan. She watched A.J.'s lips as he sucked on her clit, feeling his tongue going back and forth over it. "Put it in your mouth and twirl it around until you make it pop! Shit, I'm going to cum!" Dior moaned as her orgasm took over her body. She shuddered under A.J.'s grasped as he moved back and she squirted all over his face. She came so hard and long.

That's when Mal had enough. He began walking over just as A.J. stood up and wiped his face. Mal looked at the dresser and noticed condoms. Where they came from, he didn't know, but he grabbed one and put it on quickly. As A.J. was standing there, Mal just bumped him out of the way, positioning his dick to her pussy. He grabbed her legs, pulling her to the edge of the bed and dipping, preparing for entrance. He pushed and was surprised that it didn't just simply go in. While he was working on going in, A.J. had his dick in her face. Dior opened her mouth to take him in. Mal pushed his way in and damn near lost all control.

"Ummmm!"

"Damn!"

"Oh shit!"

Everybody moaned in unison for different reasons. A.J. moaned because Dior's mouth was so warm and wet on his dick. Mal moaned because her pussy felt so warm wrapped tightly around his dick. Dior moaned because she was in heaven. She had a big dick in her pussy and a big dick in her mouth.

Mal was standing on the side of the bed, going in and out of her pussy. His strokes were deep first and then long. A.J was on the bed face fucking Dior, but Dior was up for the challenge. She sat up on her elbows for better leverage. She wrapped her hand around his dick and began to stroke it while sucking the head.

"Damn, girl, suck that shit!" A.J. just looked down at her, making his dick disappear in her mouth with no gag. She pulled her head back, looked at him, and spit on his dick, leaving a trail of spit from her lip to his dick. Then she went back to work, going hard. She was working A.J. while Mal was fucking the shit out of her.

Mal was going in hard and slow. His technique was A-1. "Grrrrrr!" Mal let out a grunt. *Her pussy is dangerous!* he couldn't stop thinking. She had a hell of a shot on her. She was so tight, he couldn't believe that shit. He just looked at his dick going in and out of her pussy, coated with so much of her juices on it, and it added to his satisfaction.

"Oh shit, shit. I'm about to cum, girl. Open up!" A.J. yelled.

Mal looked up just as A.J. began shooting cum straight into Dior's open mouth, and she took every drop, looking Mal straight in his eye as she swallowed.

Mal had stopped stroking as A.J. started to get dressed, going in his pocket and placing a bundle of money next to Dior's purse. A.J. looked up only to catch Dior's eyes on what he was doing. He just smirked. That was one thing he liked about her. No matter how much she was into what she was doing, money was never a forgotten aspect. He grabbed the bag and walked out the door. He had to go meet Jessica downstairs so they could take this trip to see Mal's connect.

Mal turned Dior over and pushed her shoulders down. He had to sit back and observe for a few seconds, because that was a sight worth observing. Out of nowhere, he just rammed his dick in her pussy from the back.

"Ummmmm!" Dior just moaned.

He was thrusting. In and out his dick went. He spread her cheeks apart, and there was still ass in the way. He loved it. Her ass jiggled with every movement.

Dior had enough of letting him take the lead, so she got off her forearms, laying her hands flat on the bed. She began to throw that shit back hard as he held her hips.

"Um um ummmmm!" Dior couldn't help but moan. She was in her favorite position. She waited until he was deep in, and when her ass was on his stomach, she made it jump ridiculously.

"Oh shit! Damn!" Mal moaned he began smacking Dior's ass.

This really turned Dior on. She started going crazy, ramming her pussy on his dick relentlessly. He knew she was close.

"I'm about to cum!" Dior announced just in the nick of time.

"Oh shit!" Mal replied as he felt her shudder, noticing how wet she got and how wet she got him. He had to make sure she didn't urinate, because she came that much. All of this brought him to his point of no return.

"Fuck!" Mal yelled out as he came deep inside of her. He gently pulled out and went to the bathroom.

Dior was well satisfied but relieved. She liked sex when she was pushed to her limits, and that seemed impossible to not occur when she was with two men. Her eyes were closed until she heard the bathroom door open.

"Guess I got something better than your number huh?" Mal announced smugly as he buckled his pants.

Dior held her blank expression while she responded, "Guess you did!" She walked in the bathroom.

All Mal could do was shake his head. He knew he just fucked the shit out of her, but she still looked at him like he wasn't shit. *This bitch is something different.*

"Fuck it!" Mal said aloud in response to his thoughts.

He knew she wouldn't come out until he left, so he went in his jeans and grabbed all the money out of his right pocket. He looked down at it. He was too lazy to count any money out. His thoughts took over. *Since she thinking I'm some broke-ass little nigga, she can have this shit.* He took his thumb over his money. He knew it was no more than ten racks. He wasn't tripping on funky-ass $10,000.

Speaking of which, he was going to have to call Mike later, his plug in Kentucky, to make sure A.J.'s and Jessica's asses made it. A.J. was his boy, but he was a runner, and that was all he would be because he was a fuckup. Mal and Eron had to run shit and make sure the money was in a constant flow, so he didn't make no more out-of-town trips unless there was an obscene amount of money on the floor.

Damn, let me get up out of here. Mal began walking out the door, pausing at the bathroom door, hearing that the shower was on. Mal quickly envisioned Dior's wet booty, making him push on the door.

"Ummm!" As Dior moaned, Mal opened the door. Damn, she just had two dicks in her less than an hour ago, and she was horny all over again.

Looking through the steaming door, he saw the silhouette of Dior's body, causing an immediate response from his dick. He watched her work her pussy, but what he heard next not only surprised him but took him over the edge. As Dior worked her clit, she brought herself to a climax.

"Damn, Jamal!" Dior let out an exaggerated moan.

Mal couldn't take it, so he went to the shower door, pulling it open.

"Did you enjoy the show?" Dior asked a surprised Mal.

Mal couldn't even answer. His dick was irritated because of his jeans acting as a constraint. He simply grabbed her hand, helping her out of the shower, and his face dove into her neck. He was like a monster possessed. He trailed down her neck with his tongue, causing her to shiver. He immediately used his hand to butterfly her pussy and began to play with her clit.

"Ummm!" Dior let out a soft moan.

Almost like a light switched, he changed up the mood, getting rough and raw. Mal took one hand, grabbing her hair and pulling her head back, and he began biting her neck.

Dior let out a gasp. She was so turned on.

He picked her up, sitting her on the sink. It was there that he pushed her titties together and began to savagely lick and bite on her nipples.

"Oooo!" Dior was in heaven. Rough was the only way she wanted it. Before she knew it, he was sticking his dick in her, hitting her spot with his first stroke.

Mal was tripping because her pussy was snug. She had that snap back for real.

"Damn!" Mal slipped and let out as he picked her up, carrying her out of the bathroom and into the bedroom. *She got some good-ass pussy!* Mal laid her on the bed, pushing her legs back and slowing stroking her, watching as his dick went in and out of her pussy.

Dior grabbed his arms, trying to tame his strokes. He was hitting the G-spot with every hit. Dior began losing it. "Oh, shit!" She let out a series of different moans. This was causing Mal to lose control. Since her legs were already pushed back, he grabbed her legs so he could stand up while he hit it.

"Umm. Damn. Oh my God!" Dior was more than surprised that he had her like this, almost effortlessly.

He placed her back to the wall, pushing her legs all the way up and back. Dior glanced up, looking at her feet touching the wall. This turned her on so much. Little did she know, Mal too was turned on, looking at the length of her legs going straight over her shoulder.

Mal had her pinned to the wall. She had nowhere to run. *She thinks she's slick!* Mal knew the game that Dior was playing. She kept tightening her pussy muscles on him, but he was breaking through that shit, tearing her shit down, but what Mal didn't know was that was what Dior liked. It's what she loved. *Slow stroking? Leave that shit to R&B niggas.* Dior loved to be fucked hard in a way that only street niggas could do. All that rough, smack ya ass, pull ya hair, biting, and all that shit.

"Ohhhhh! I'm about to come! Oh shit! Mmmmmm!" Dior alerted him. Mal started to hit it harder and more relentlessly. He was beating that shit up in every sense of the words. Mal felt her shiver and shake. He watched her orgasm take over her body. This made him beat it even harder if that was possible. Mal was drilling his dick into Dior's pussy with unforeseen strength. She looked corrupted with her eyes rolling in the back of her head.

What she said next was what surprised him. "I want you to finish from the back." It was then that as he stroked, she was squirting. "Ummmmmmmm!" Dior was practically screaming. "Yesssssss. Don't stop! Pleaseeeee!"

It was taking Mal everything he had not to cum, so he pulled out, helping her to the bed. At this point, her orgasm subsided. She let go of his hand, placing both knees on the bed. Mal watched in awe as her ass bounced wildly. It was natural movement. He was stuck.

Dior's hands and knees were on the bed as she looked over her shoulder. "Are you going to finish or nah?" Dior asked with a smirk, causing Mal to smirk because he knew was caught trying to procrastinate and stop himself from cumming.

"I got this!" Mal replied, using her cum from his stomach to lubricate his dick. He placed each hand on each check. He bent down, licked her ass, and smacked it as hard as he could.

"Umm, smack it again!" Dior demanded, and Mal obliged as he placed the head of his dick to the opening of her pussy. Dior immediately pushed back on it.

"Whoa, baby girl!" *Did I just say that ho-ass shit? Oh well, her pussy shouldn't be this damn good.* Mal was surprised that some weak shit like that made it out of his mouth. Sure, good pussy was easy to come by, but great pussy wasn't. The women he came across didn't make him want to make sure they were pleased.

He in my world now! Dior was in the zone as she went slowly at first and would speed up at any given moment. He just held on for the ride.

"Damn, girl, fuck it. Do ya thang, baby!"

"Ummmmm." All he got in response were moans from Dior.

She continuously threw that ass back hard. He had to hold on tight to maintain balance. She went around and around while his dick was deep inside her. That "Too Short" song came to mind when he said, "Bet she can't wiggle like that with a dick in her." He clearly hadn't had the opportunity to fuck Dior. She had her ass clapping on his dick. Dior popped her pussy on his dick with ease. *This bitch is something different! Good-ass pussy, too!* "Damn, Dior, I'm about to cum!"

Dior knew that once she got him to hit her from the back, he wouldn't be able to last that long. Dior hurriedly jumped off his dick, turning and placing it in her mouth. She began to suck hard and fast. She loved the way a hard dick felt in her mouth, especially when it was about release semen. She sucked deep so that his dick was touching the back of her throat.

"Oh shit, damn! Here I cummmmm!" Mal went crazy face fucking her, gripping the back of her neck. A typical girl couldn't take this, but typical wasn't in Dior's description. He shot his load deep in her throat. Dior took his dick slightly out of her mouth so he could see his cum leave his dick and enter her mouth. That shit was a major turn-on for Mal. When his nut left his dick, he watched it land all in and around Dior's mouth.

Mal looked down. The sight before him was picture perfect. She took him for all he had. She began sucking and jacking him off.

"Damn!" Mal was surprised that she sucked everything he had out of him and kept going like it was nothing.

"Mmmmm." Dior swallowed every drop.

Mal smiled as he looked down at her. "You are something different!"

"So I've been told," Dior replied as Mal walked into the bathroom.

Dior just lay back on the bed as her thoughts ran rampant. Damn, I need a drink. *Maybe I'ma go out and have one. Shit, that was a little too good. I need a nap.* She felt herself drifting into a satisfied sleep.

"Ahem!" Mal clearing his throat made Dior open her eyes.

"You gon' chill here for a—"

Mal's phone rang: "They asked my name, but he told 'em John Doe—" He interrupted his Rick Ross ringtone because he answered the phone so quick.

"Yeah, nigga, y'all made it?"

"No, we haven't made it just yet. We are about two hours out."

"Damn, what's taking so long? You know what, just get there. I mean why the fuck is it taking you so long? All right, look, just call Mike on the 404 number when you get close so he can look out for y'all. Call me when it's done," Mal said, ending the call. Then he finished his previous question to Dior. "My bad, but are you gon' chill here?"

"Yeah, I'm tired," Dior responded with a yawn.

"All right, well I'm having a party tomorrow at this new club, Club LAX, downtown. You should come."

"I don't know, maybe."

"Um, you something else. All right, be careful out here," Mal said, shaking his head.

"You too!" Dior replied, restless. She waited until she heard the door shut before she drifted off to a comfortable sleep.

What a night!

Chapter Eleven

I got my change up; they looking like they surprised.
Niggas hatin' on me hard 'cause my paper right.

The sound of Dior's phone ringing woke her from her deep sleep.

"Hello!"

"Ewww. Wake up!" said Ashley, Dior's cousin, who stayed in Atlanta. They grew up more like sisters. Ashley was the only person Dior would let get close to her. That was by default, because Ashley went to Atlanta to attend Spelman. She received her degree and would be going to law school the following fall. Dior and Ashley were far from dumb. Dior was building her credentials. She just liked to fuck. She did what most bitches would sneak around to do.

"Man, don't start! It's too late!" Dior replied, grumpy, like she always did after being woken up.

"Man, I'm at your house. Where are you?"

"Are you really? Why didn't you tell me that you were coming? What time is it?" Dior wondered as she sat up, beginning to get dressed.

"I was trying to surprise you. It's four a.m. My flight landed at midnight. Sincere came and got me from the airport. More like kidnapped me." Sincere and Ashley had a crazy relationship. Bottom line was whenever she needed him he was there and vice versa.

Sincere was black as night. He was gorgeous. He wore his curly hair in a low taper. He had blemish-free skin and stood at six feet five inches. He had bitches falling at his feet. When Ashley was in town, bitches knew to not even look in dude's direction. He played all day if he knew you. If you didn't know him, he was most dominating. You wouldn't think he was as cool as he was.

"Shut up. I'm not far. I'll be there in like twenty minutes," Dior announced, hanging up the phone. She placed on her shoes and headed toward the valet. She jumped on I-96, which took her to her Redford home. She had to stay away from where she played.

She got out of her car, grabbing her bags to head in the house. *Damn, I'm glad I gave her ass a key.*

Before Dior could even open the door, Ashley was screaming and running into her arms. "Oh my God, I missed you!" Ashley made it known by the thrill in her voice.

"Here you go with that soft shit!" Dior retorted. She always played the tough role, but she really missed her sister/cousin. Dior didn't mess with too many females, so her cousin was her only true friend.

"Here you go with that tough shit!" Ashley replied in her smart tone as they walked into Dior's kitchen. "But anyway, Sincere said he wants us to party with him tonight. You down?"

As Dior sat down at her kitchen table, she looked at Ashley like she was crazy. "This is my cousin's first day home, and you really think I'm not going to party with her? Where are we going?" Dior wondered.

Ashley replied, "He said some new club, called Club LAX. His boy owns it."

Dior just burst out laughing. "Oh really? Ummm, we are most definitely in the building."

"What was that about?" Ashley wondered.

"Oh, this one nigga I met and fucked yesterday wanted me to come down there. Welp, guess I have to go now," Dior faked, not wanting to go.

"Oh, hush, like you didn't want to. I know some money was on the floor." Ashley knew better. She and Dior both believed that as long as a woman had a pussy, that woman should never go broke. These women were nothing average. They were the best of both worlds. Ashley was a red-bone, short, thick woman. She had light brown, exotic eyes and some of the clearest skin. Her lips were big. Her body was sick. She had succulent C-cup breasts with an unbelievably tiny waistline leading into her fat ass.

"Come on now, I learned from the best. Niggas only treat you how you act, right?" Dior asked. She expected this from Ashley. She had love for no nigga except Sincere. But when it came to money she'd even say fuck him too. Not as in doing something grimy to him for money. Sincere never let it get like that, because his money stretched to wherever Ashley went.

"This is true. So tell me this, did you fuck one nigga or two niggas?" Ashley wondered with a smile.

"You know me so well. You know A.J.?"

Ashley nodded.

"Him and his friend Mal. Mal is the one who wants me to come down to the club. Man, it was so good, I think I came harder with Mal by himself, and he paid! His movements say money. Not all loud like A.J. but chill. Just the way I like it."

"Wait, I think Sincere said something about niggas named Mal and Eron owning the club."

"Oh, really?" Dior wasn't surprised. She loved a hustling-ass nigga. Being broke was never an attractive feature on anybody, male or female.

"Jackpot. All right. I'm about to go to sleep. Wake me up when it's time to go," Ashley said as she walked to the bedroom that she used when she was in town. "Oh, Sincere supposed to come back."

"What you telling me for?" Dior asked. Sincere and Ashley were kind of a package deal. He was a busy man, but when Ashley came into town, he was always near. Dior loved him because he didn't judge her by the things that she did. He was Ashley's shooter and vice versa. It was nothing for him to make something happen for Ashley. Distance didn't matter. Whenever he decided to, he was on his way to the ATL.

Dior decided to follow her lead. Shit, she needed some rest too. She did have a long-ass day.

Chapter Twelve

"Wake up! Wake up!" Dior heard Ashley's annoying-ass voice. She decided to be stubborn.

"Aye, man, you ugly when you sleep!" Dior's eyes popped open at the sound of a man's voice.

Ashley and Sincere erupted in laughter because they scared Dior. Sincere loved anything that had to do with Ashley, including Dior. He looked at Dior as his sister. Whenever she needed something, he was her Johnny-on-the-spot.

"Get out of my room. I hate y'all!" Dior made known with laughter in her voice.

"Nigga, it's seven p.m. and you still in the bed," Sincere shouted.

"This fool want to take us to Andiamo before we go to the club, so hurry up!" Ashley told her.

"Oh damn, y'all dressed, too. Here I come." Dior replied, getting out of bed. *What to wear?* Dior went to her closet, picking a black-and-white dress and red "come fuck me" heels. She headed to the shower, glancing in the mirror on her way. *Time for some more dick.* To Dior, dick made a good day better. She hopped in the shower, taking the time to moisturize her skin.

Banging on the door shook her a little bit. "Hurry up!" Sincere's crazy ass shouting through the door didn't surprise her. He didn't play that shit. He hated waiting.

Dior yanked the door open dressed in her robe. "Move, nigga! Here I come."

Sincere just shook his head, going back into Ashley's room.

Dior got herself together quick, and before they knew it, they were climbing into Sincere's 2012 Durango. He always had a new car. That was just how he did it. It was impossible to keep up with his cars.

They pulled up to Andiamo at 9:30. They had a nice dinner, talking about everybody who darkened the restaurant's doorstep.

"All right, ladies, time to go!" Sincere announced as he paid the check, proceeding to get out of his seat. He had to meet up with his homeboy Mal to cop some Mary Jane. Mal and Eron kept the best Kush in the city. He helped the ladies up and walked behind them, getting envious looks from the men in the restaurant.

They took the twenty-minute drive downtown to the airport-themed club. They pulled up, and in no time the valet was opening the doors for them.

"What up, Sincere?" Neither Ashley nor Dior was surprised that the valet knew him. Sincere knew everybody in Detroit.

"What up, boy? Let me stay in the front," Sincere replied, greeting and informing the valet all at once.

"No problem. I got you big time!" the valet replied, taking the two bills from Sincere's hand.

They walked to the door of the club. The bouncer shook Sincere's hand, and they were in. They proceeded to the VIP, getting stares from both men and women. Men were in awe because Sincere had two bad bitches with him, fitting any breathing man's taste. Women were straight-up envious because Ashley was in town, and they knew to stay far away. They sat down with Sincere, immediately ordering three bottles. Ashley ordered some 1738, and Dior ordered some Grey Goose and cranberry.

In no time their drinks were back, and they were indulging. Dior was a dancer. She enjoyed it. "Come on, Ash, you already know!"

Ashley got up. "Let's do it!"

"Do y'all thing. I'll be around," Sincere said, grabbing his bottle and going on a search to find his boy who owned the club.

Dior and Ashley barely made it to the dance floor with everybody stopping them to say one thing or another.

A cut from one of the great Atlanta rappers, T.I., had the club rocking. None of the females in the club were fucking with Dior and Ashley. Some came close, but that didn't count. They were grinding and winding their bodies to the beat and had niggas mesmerized. A couple of them tried to get a dance, but the girls just pushed them away.

They went crazy when a Yo Gotti cut came on. They started cutting up. While Ashley dropped it low and picked it up slow, Dior pulled her dress down and bent over, making her ass roll and shake to the beat. When she was coming back up, she noticed that Sincere was now with Ashley. Sincere loved to watch Ashley dance. Dior kept doing her thing and bent back over, noticing some Gucci sneakers approaching her, and in no time she felt a hard dick on her ass. Turning around to see who the clown was, she was shocked to see Mal looking so good.

"You was about to go off, huh?" Mal smirked.

"You already know you got to pay to play," Dior said with a straight face.

"I know all too well. I'd pay again, too," Mal felt the need to let her know.

"Mal, man, what you doing all on my cousin?" Sincere asked as he approached them.

"Aw, man, I ain't even know she was your peoples." Mal was shocked, but he really ain't give a fuck whose cousin

Dior was. He was on li'l mama. He did find it funny that he never met Dior even though he had been rocking with the nigga Sin for a while. Sin was his dog. They did business, but they would just kick it and shoot the breeze, too.

Sincere made introductions. "Aye, Mal, this is my girl, Ashley. Ashley, this my nigga I was telling you about. He owns this club. Oh, you already know Ashley's cousin, Dior." As Mal shook Ashley's hand, he just laughed at Sincere trying to be funny. "Oh, and I know she know you 'cause you was all up on that thang."

Everybody started laughing. "Shut up, stupid. Damn, Sincere, you really know everybody," a frustrated Dior replied. Sincere was very observant. Nothing got by him.

"You already know," Sincere retorted, kissing all on Ashley's neck.

Mal had been staring at Dior the whole time. He wanted her now. "Dior, come up to my office with me!" Mal said with his desire for her in his tone as he whispered in her ear. Mal didn't even wait for a reply. He grabbed her hand, leading her through the club to his upstairs office. They walked in. There was a huge two-way mirror showing the entire club. This was the first thing Dior noticed.

"We can see them, and they can't see us?" Dior asked, intrigued.

"At least until I flip this switch," Mal answered, flipping a switch and making them visible to the club. This turned Dior on to no end. She immediately pushed him on top of his desk, releasing his dick. Dior began sucking his dick like her life depended on it.

"Damn, just like that huh?" A defeated Mal looked down at her. She never answered. Dior looked up, taking her mouth off his dick and leaving a trail of spit from her mouth to his dick.

"Oh shit!" Mal was in a state of euphoria. He grabbed the back of her head, beginning to fuck her face at a slow but steady pace then quickly speeding up. In no time she felt him tensing up. She knew he was close

"Fuck! Damn, I'm about to cum!" Mal shouted, releasing his seed down Dior's throat. She swallowed every drop. Mal opened his eyes, looking down at the club watching them.

"I'm about to fuck the shit out of you." Mal picked her up off the floor and placed her on the desk. Pulling her dress up over her waist, he put her legs on his shoulders and began to fuck her hard. He picked her up to give the people of the club a side view.

"Oh shit. Um." Dior's moans were all over the place. She couldn't help it. *Mal's dick should be bronzed and given out as an award.*

"Damn, girl, you got some good-ass pussy!" Mal grumbled as he watched his dick go in and out. He began to fuck her harder and rougher. He was shocked when even in that position she was throwing her pussy at him. It was then that he slid her off his dick, and turning her ass to him, he stuck it in her ass.

"Oh shit! Go in hard and fast," a distressed Dior let out. The pain that she felt in her ass was indescribable, but the feeling was so good that it was overwhelming.

Mal took his dick out, and in one swift motion, he began fucking her ass.

"Oh. Oh. Oh!" Dior was bucking and going wild. Mal took her in front of the mirror, so they were looking at the club people. All Mal could do was shake with his groaning inaudible terms. This shit was erotic as hell.

"Oh my God. Here I come!" Dior told Mal, but even that couldn't prepare him for what came covering his dick and the mirror before them. He noticed that the people below them were in awe of the amount of juices that covered the glass. All of the juices coming from Dior were astronomical, more than enough to make a man feel like "the man." Mal didn't even let her come down. He was ready to cum, so he put his dick in her pussy.

"It's my turn to cum now!" Mal told Dior as he began to fuck her from behind, hitting her spot repeatedly. He was so rough that he could no longer hold his groaning in.

"Ummmmm." While Mal was speaking gibberish, Dior was screaming because of the beating he was giving her pussy. It was the best type of pain.

"Fuuuuuucccccck." Mal came deep in her pussy. They both began to shake. Dior came again.

"Ummmm!"

They began getting themselves together. Mal flipped the switch to the mirror. As he pulled his pants up, he went in his right pocket and then stuffed money into her purse. Dior watched the whole scene. For pussy that good, Mal didn't mind paying.

"Thank you, Mal."

"I got you!" Mal said as Dior walked ahead of him out of the office. Mal only shook his head, watching her ass bounce as she walked down the steps. He was ready to go again. They finally made it into the club, getting a round of applause. Dior and Mal paid it no attention. Mal got stopped while Dior kept walking.

"Good show," Ashley and Sincere said simultaneously.

"Y'all so childish! But I aim to please," Dior smartly responded. Dior wasn't sneaking. She was upfront about her shit. That was something only the real could appreciate.

They proceeded to walk out of the club without a problem until Dior heard something in the crowd.

"She a busto!" a weak-ass, hating-ass bitch decided to be bold enough to say. In the hood, a busto wasn't a city in Italy. A busto was a runner, a freak bitch, a female who didn't mind getting down. A busto usually left with a wet ass and empty pockets. That by no means described a bitch like Dior.

Dior looked back. "I'm Dior, the Busto Bitch! Just know this: you'll hate this week, and you'll hate next week. Both weeks I get paid." She pranced out of the club without a care in the world.

Mal watched on, digging Dior's whole style.

Chapter Thirteen

Back at the restaurant, everybody finished their food and was tuned in like Channel 2 Fox News. Even Mal sat back, amazed by the type of female Dior was.

"So that's what it is. Many people judge me. I'm used to it. But through it all, I'm on my money chase."

"Man, you ain't got to make a disclaimer. I'm a grown-ass man. I for damn sure don't need a good girl," Jamal stated matter-of-factly. "I want to get to know you more."

Dior looked on, loving that Jamal wasn't intimidated by her choices. Most men were. *This could be interesting.*

Eron jumped in. "Well, I guess we'll see you tomorrow at graduation."

Dior was confused. "So that's all you got to say?"

"Shit, what do I supposed to say? Mal a grown-ass man. I trust his judgment. Shit, I know bitches who do more for less. I will say this though, you need to end whatever ties you have to that nigga A.J."

"There are no ties, so that won't be a problem. I just won't talk to him or answer his calls. Matter of fact, if he should call, I'll just let him know that ain't shit up. It's just that simple and plain."

Aaliyah chimed in. "Who did you think we were? We all got skeletons in our closet. Now, do you have plans after graduation?"

"Not really. Ashley and her dude coming. I think we just gon' play it by ear."

"Okay, cool. Y'all can come to Eron's mom's house for a barbeque they are throwing in honor of my graduation. It's going to be a small gathering. Afterward, we're going to head to the club to top off our day. Are you with it?"

"That sounds like a plan to me. That is, if Mal doesn't mind me hanging out him and his family."

"Come on, na. That's a question you ain't even got to ask me." Jamal was so cool as he quoted T.I. in the Young Jeezy song "Bang."

Aaliyah was excited. Her face lit up. Eron loved the way Aaliyah's face looked when she happy.

"Okay then cool. Guess we'll see you tomorrow then."

Everybody hugged saying their good-byes. Eron and Aaliyah made their way out of the restaurant, noticing that Dior and Jamal didn't budge.

"Guess they still had things to discuss."

"Come on, nosey," Eron said as he ushered Aaliyah into the car.

"Damn!"

"What the fuck?"

"It's crazy how things playing out. But anyway."

Chapter Fourteen

Mal and Dior

"So why haven't I seen you?" When Dior left the club, Mal had no way of getting touch with her. Through everything they never exchanged numbers.

"I just figured you would find me if you needed to." Dior didn't know where this shyness was coming from, but she started to feel intimidated by Mal. She wasn't sure what she was feeling, but Mal stayed on her mind, and she didn't like it.

What Dior didn't know was that she too had Mal in a confused state. Why would he want a bitch like Dior? Mal did his thang in the streets. He was a hungry-ass nigga, but the thing that separated him from other niggas was that he didn't mind putting in the work. Big E laid the blueprint for him and Eron to follow.

Mal didn't want a "good bitch." He needed a bitch who understood the ups and downs that came with the game. He wanted a teammate. No, he didn't want or need Dior popping pussy for the next nigga. Mal would make sure she was past good. He needed a rider. He wanted a bitch who would bust her guns if it came to that. Bottom line, the hustle he saw in Dior was admirable. Who was he to judge her hustle? Hell, he wasn't exactly legal, almost. But almost didn't count to the law.

"You right. I did find you shopping. I don't like that, so let's fix this now. Put your number in my phone." Mal handed her his phone.

Dior laughed, but she wasn't stupid. She did what she was told. Mal snatched his phone from Dior and immediately called her phone. "Just so you can have it."

Dior smirked. "Got it. So what's up? You got something else to do?" Dior asked. She hadn't had grade A quality dick since the last time they fucked.

"Nah. I ain't busy. My work is done for the day. What you got in mind?"

"Meet me at Motor City. Room 1210."

Mal started laughing immediately because it was the same room that they were in the last time. "All right, I'll meet you there."

The two parted ways. No more words were needed. Dior and Mal both knew what was up.

Mal knocked on the hotel door. He made a pit stop on the way to the room to see his mom. It was a must for him to check on the home front, especially since his mom refused to move out of the hood. The only good he saw in her still living in the same house that they lived in since they moved to Detroit was that Eron's mom was just as stubborn. They still looked out for each other, probably even more since Big E was locked up in the federal penitentiary.

The door opened, and the sight before him left him speechless. Dior quickly turned around, leaving Mal to take in her bare ass.

"Damn."

Jamal was stunned by the scene before him. Dior didn't speak one word. Dior walked to the middle of the room and pulled a portable pole out of a Cirillia's bag. Jamal finally sat on the bed and began to roll up.

This woman is full of surprises. I'ma sit back and enjoy the show.

Dior continued to unfold the pole while she stole glances of Jamal. The nigga even made rolling a blunt look good. Dior finally had the pole tightened and suctioned to the wall and ceiling. Dior pressed play on her iPod and their situation played with a beat to it in the form of T.I.'s song "Freak Though."

Immediately Mal knew the track. He'd listened to it himself and was amazed at how perfect the song was for their particular situation. T.I. spoke about a chick he was digging, but the hood said she got around. Of course, a typical man would be derailed by the rumors of the chick being a ho. But T.I. was embracing the challenge, and so was Mal. It would take a real nigga to deal with Dior. Dior just needed to be tamed and paid. Mal wouldn't tolerate disrespect about her.

Mal sat smoking his blunt and watching Dior work the pole. He was amazed. Dior could've easily taken her talents to South Beach, Miami. Dior grabbed the pole with both hands, dipping in a squat position, and started twerking her ass checks.

Mal couldn't even get a word out. He was thoroughly pleased. The girls from the "Twerk Team" would've easily made a spot on the squad for Dior's talents. She went to the beat. One cheek. Both cheeks. Left cheek and then right cheek and then simultaneously. Dior attempted to do more tricks, but Mal had had enough. He got up, taking off his shirt on the way. Dior was shocked but didn't show it. Mal grabbed her, standing her in the upright position up against the pole.

"Why are you teasing a real nigga?" Mal didn't give Dior a chance to answer his question before he began shooting off a statement. "That shit was sexy though. Ain't nothing like your own personal dancer." Mal's lips immediately found Dior's neck as he unhooked her bra.

"Ummm!" Dior was amazed that Mal being so close to her turned her on to no end. His lips touching her was an added bonus.

Mal immediately went to her titties. He sucked and licked her titties like it was his last meal. Mal grabbed at her ass as he moved her away from the pole and toward the bed. He pushed her on the bed. Dior was in a state of shock. Mal handled her with so much desire. A person could lie and try to fight off the way they may be feeling, but sex was a surefire way for your emotions to tell your truth.

Something snapped in Dior. She felt the need to show him that as fucked up as their situation was, there was something that she wanted to explore. Dior quickly unbuckled his pants, releasing the dragon. Her mouth instantly watered at the sight of his gorgeous dick. Dior wasted no time surrounding his dick with her mouth.

"Whoa! Shit!" Mal was confused. *Wasn't I running the show?*

Mal just lay there as he watched Dior make his dick disappear. Her movements were admirable. Dior turned into a bobblehead on the dick.

Slurp! Slurp!

"Damn!' Mal was a goner. It got so good for him that he gripped her head, using the other hand for leverage as he pumped in and out of her mouth at a rapid pace. Mal felt his dick hitting the back of her mouth. The scene itself was erotic as fuck. The way the spit fell from her lubricating his dick was too much for Mal. Mal had to stop her.

"I don't want to cum like that. Sit on this muthafucka."

Dior wasn't one for disappointment. She snatched her panties off as she climbed on top of Mal. Mal picked up her panties.

"Damn, they are soaked."

"That's all you." Dior wasn't lying. Sucking Mal's dick had her dripping wet. To have him in such a vulnerable state was so exciting. Dior eased his dick into her hot awaiting vagina from the back. It took them both by surprise.

"Ahhh."

"Oh, shit!"

Mal's hands immediately went to rub her ass, almost like a magnetic force was linking the two. He caressed her ass like it was precious. The sight of Dior arching her back, looking over her shoulder, and riding him was picture perfect. One would've thought she had "equestrian" on her resume. Dior's ass looked to have a mind of its own. The way it moved while her hips went up and down was out of this world.

"Shit, Jamal, I'm about to cum."

"Cum on so I can cum," Mal coaxed Dior. He didn't know how much longer he could hold off before he exploded.

Dior started to buck like crazy. She extended her arm so that she lay as flat as she possibly could, working only her ass up and down. In no time she was releasing a huge orgasm.

"Oh shit. Shit. I'm cumming!" It showed too. Dior looked like she got the shivers. In between watching her ass and feeling her warm pussy dripping wet from her orgasm, Mal was a goner. In no time he was meeting her at the finish line.

Chapter Fifteen

"Now, I can tell y'all about the graduation day. I feel like I can make sense of the day now."

Eron woke Aaliyah up, kissing all over her face. Muah! Muah! Muah! Muah! "Get up! My baby a graduate! But she doesn't want to wake up."

Aaliyah rolled over, covering her face with her arm. She knew that she needed to get up, but she was tired. The stress of finally completing college and making preparations with Eron's mother was getting to her.

Eron started shaking Aaliyah. "Get your ass up."

"I'm up. Damn," Aaliyah snapped, getting up and heading straight to the shower.

"You a ol' evil muthafucker. I'm about to go take care of some business. I'll see you at the school."

"Okay." Aaliyah hopped into the shower, feeling so drained and a little overwhelmed. She made it a quick shower because she needed to get her hair done at nine.

I might as well get dressed now. It'll be easier than trying to get dressed at the shop or the school.

Aaliyah had an eerie feeling about the day, but she just counted it toward missing her mother. She just got dressed in a Herve Lager dress and Yves Saint Laurent pumps. Combing her hair down, she knew that she wouldn't feel the full effect until Mike worked his magic on her hair.

Aaliyah peeked through the blinds, and the black S550 Mercedes-Benz was parked in the driveway. *Guess I can drive that.* Eron would usually pull out a car of the three for her to drive before he left to go to "work."

Aaliyah hopped in the car and smiled at the sight before her. Not only did she see a big Louis Vuitton bag, but she saw her cap and gown hanging in the back seat. She just had to pick up the phone and call Eron.

"Don't be calling now! Yo' ass just had attitude." Eron was pushing the bitch Jessica off of him. He originally went over there because he wanted her to take a couple trips OT. She played hard to get, of course, but she came around.

"Thank you, baby! I love it! You are the man!" Aaliyah exclaimed as she pulled out of the driveway, stealing a glance at the Louis Vuitton Damier Belmont bag.

"You deserve that and more. You're my graduate," Eron declared, looking Jessica in the eye and daring her to say some dumb shit.

"All right, love, I'll see you later." Aaliyah hung up as she got out of the car to lock the box in the trunk. In Detroit, if a nigga felt like there was some money in your car, they had no problem busting your window to get it. Nah, a school graduation wasn't safe either. Detroit was full of grimy niggas. If a nigga wanted what you had, they did whatever to make it happen.

Aaliyah pulled out the driveway heading to Salon DNA to see Mike H. By the time she got to the shop. She had an hour to get in and out. Aaliyah was buzzed into the shop.

"Hey, boo," Mike greeted her. Mike was one of the coldest stylists in the D. He was humble and great at what he did. There were other great stylists in Detroit, and Mike did their hair too. He was definitely their favorite stylist.

"Hey, Mike." As she walked closer to Mike's styling chair, she saw the person he was finishing up. "Well, hello, Ms. Dior!"

Dior blushed. "Hello to you, Ms. Lady. You look gorgeous as ever."

"Nah. Not yet. Mike ain't put his touch on it yet. You look really pretty also." Dior really did look amazing in her off-white knee-length fitted dress topped off with silver accessories and pink Gucci peep-toe pumps. Mike styled her hair in an out-cold bob.

Mike chimed in. "I see y'all finally crossed paths. Aaliyah, I been telling Dior about you for the longest. Y'all remind me of each other."

"He has been telling me about you. He speaks highly of you."

"That's flattering. Thanks, Mike. Yeah, we are definitely going to hang out a bit. We can definitely shop. We got that part." Aaliyah snickered as Mike ushered Dior out of the chair and Aaliyah into it.

"All right, thanks, Mike. Aaliyah, congratulations. I'll see you at the school."

They said their good-byes and Dior was out the door. It didn't take Mike long to whip Aaliyah's hair in big curls. She was now graduation ready!

Aaliyah and Dior sat in the same section, waiting for their names to be called. The graduates and their families had to sit through five guest speakers, over 400 undergrad students, and over 1,000 graduate students.

"Aaliyah Banks, bachelor of science in computer information systems."

"Dior Mancill, bachelor of social work, BSW."

Everything said after or before their names was a blur. Dior and Aaliyah gave each other a hug and went in search of their families.

"Congratulations!"

Their heads snapped around. Dior just shook her head at Ashley racing over to her.

"Thank you, baby!"

Aaliyah watched the transaction and couldn't help but feel slight jealousy. She missed her mother. She would've been so proud and pushing her every step of the way.

Eron stood back with Mal and Sincere chopping it up. They all went way back. It was always love and loyalty. They would sometimes do business together. Eron looked at Aaliyah's face and immediately knew what she was thinking about.

"Congratulations, love." Eron came up to Aaliyah, hugging her tight. "Baby, she is smiling down on you. Just be happy today. And fuck that nigga Calvin. He's not your fucking daddy."

Aaliyah just shook her head. "You right. I'm back."

"All right. All right, break that shit up! Let me give my sister a hug!" Jamal exclaimed, knowing that if he didn't, they would be under each other all day.

"Aww. Come on, bring it in, brother. You knew you were going to get a hug."

"Uhh! Get the fuck on. Here, man!" Mal said, giving her one of two big Neiman Marcus bags.

"Oooohhhh!" Aaliyah couldn't wait to open it, but they were only surrounded by grass. "Uhhh I guess I'll just wait."

Eron interrupted and said, "Baby, you remember Sincere?"

"Yeah, I do. How are you?" Even Aaliyah had to acknowledge that Sincere was fine.

"I'm good, gorgeous. Congratulations on your accomplishments."

"Thanks, I appreciate it!"

Dior came over, walking with her cousin and appearing to be so happy. "Aaliyah, I wanted to give you a second to talk to your boo, but this is my cousin Ashley."

"Hi, Ashley, it's good to meet you."

"It's good to meet you too, Ms. Aaliyah. I hear great things, and congratulations are in order. I wish you much success."

"Thank you much."

Dior looked up at Mal. Watching the two look at each other you could see that there was something big in the making. Mal walked up to Dior.

"Congratulations," Mal said, hugging her and handing her a big Neiman Marcus bag.

Dior was shocked. Mal had just given her some money this morning. They even rode to the graduation together. After they had sex, they talked more, getting to know more about one another. They had a late dinner and breakfast. Mal and Dior had plenty in common, and by the morning they both felt that this move was worth trying out. Dior pressed the issue that she didn't want to rush.

"Thank you. I'll open it later."

"Okay, let's take pictures," Aaliyah announced. The group gathered around, posing for pictures. Everybody was genuinely happy for one another's success. It was a joyous occasion. Some old friends mixed with some new friends and people just getting to know one another. Yeah, May 12 marked a great day.

"Wow!" Aaliyah was amazed at the lengths that Tina and Jackie went through to give her a barbeque in honor of her graduating college. There were streamers and banners congratulating Aaliyah. It was beautiful. There were napkins, cups, straws, tablecloths, everything with Aaliyah's name on it. Jackie was the cook, straight down-South cooking. She was a master at anything that involved a kitchen. Here in Detroit, everybody fucked with "Motor City Soul Food." It was great food, but if you had to choose between Jackie and Motor City, it would be a tough choice. Jackie cooked everything that she ever saw Aaliyah eat. The menu consisted of ribs, steaks, pork chops, chicken, burgers, turkey burgers, hot dogs, macaroni and cheese, dressing, yams, greens, and various desserts.

"Ma, I told you, y'all ain't have to do all this, man."

"Girl, shut up. I do what I want to for mine."

Aaliyah couldn't argue with that. It made her heart smile that she always felt love over at Eron's mom's house.

From day one, Tina was always nice, but she definitely said how she felt. She was a very pretty older lady. Her wisdom spoke her age, because she sure didn't look it. Tina was a tiny woman, a brick house at four foot eleven. She had D-cup breasts, a slim waist, and a fat booty. Tina could easily pass for Eron's older sister. Since Big E was working out heavily in the penitentiary, she too fell in love with the gym. Tina was all for Big E coming home to an even better wife.

"Damn, Ma, hi to you too," Eron said, because when Aaliyah came around, he was a nonfactor. When Aaliyah and Tina first met and his mom liked her, he knew it was real, because Tina didn't like anybody. It was cool because when she met Tina, she didn't meet her as "Eron's girl," but Tina knew and voiced that it wouldn't be long before they furthered their relationship. Eron and Aaliyah both knew she was right.

"Therrrreeeee goes my baby! Correction: my graduate baby!" Aaliyah turned to look Jackie in the face. Jackie was no slouch by a long shot. She was five foot four with full B-cup breasts, a slim waist, thick thighs, and a fat booty. Jackie had a youthful look to her, but don't get it twisted. She'd let anybody know how she felt.

"Hey, Auntie baby!" Aaliyah hugged Jackie, looking over her shoulder. She saw Eron's cousin looking with a look that held so much maliciousness.

Tierra was a young, miserable, money-hungry bitch. As soon as Aaliyah met her, she rubbed her the wrong way. Eron confirmed that he didn't even trust her. He had love for her, but he didn't trust her. The girl was always "hee-hee ha-ha-ing," but something just didn't sit right with Aaliyah about her. *Yeah, I got to watch that bitch. Better safe than sorry.*

"Thanks, Auntie Jackie. Y'all are the best."

In walked Dior and Jamal into the backyard. Everybody looked shocked with Ashley and Sincere in tow. Sincere and Ashley knew most of the people since they were frequent visitors. No, he wasn't as close as Eron and Mal, but he knew that they had his back and vice versa.

"Heyyyy, Dior!" Aaliyah said, hugging Dior, hoping to make her feel comfortable under everybody's glare. Jamal didn't really bring his females around his mama at all. Mal was even surprised by his own actions.

Dior spoke into Aaliyah's ear, "Thank you." Dior didn't cower easily, but she was feeling overwhelmed by things appearing to be moving way too fast. She knew that she wouldn't be meeting his mom so soon if she weren't with the group coming together to celebrate Aaliyah's graduation.

Jackie and Tina came over, hugging Sincere and Ashley. "How are my babies doing? He better be taking care of you!"

"Man, here you go! How y'all doing? I'ma just exit stage left. Eron, ride with me to the store right quick. We got to turn up!"

Eron shook his head as he wrapped up the conversation with his uncle on the other side of the backyard.

"Boy, bye! Now, who is this graduate? Congratulations, by the way."

"Ma, this is my friend Dior. She's Ashley's cousin, and she goes to school with Aaliyah."

Jackie and Tina looked at Mal blushing. "Well, it's nice to me you, Ms. Dior. This bighead-ass boy is my son. You can call me Jackie. This is my sister, Tina, Eron's mom. Please make yourself at home. I know you got to be good people, because they all acting funny."

Dior immediately felt comfortable. "Thanks. It's good to meet you lovely ladies. I got to be honest with you. Y'all are gorgeous. I swear y'all look like y'all one of us. We can hope."

Jackie and Tina were all smiles. Mal just shook his head. "Ohhh, Lord, why you tell their hot ass that shit?"

"Boy, shut up," Tina and Jackie said in unison, causing the group to chuckle. Tina winked at Dior. "A woman after our own heart."

"Oh, niece." Jackie turned toward Aaliyah. "Guess what Jackie had made?"

"What else did y'all do?"

"Jackie had somebody fill the iPod with a whole bunch of T.I. songs. Since that's all our children like to listen to."

Aaliyah's face lit up, looking at Mal. He was already on the way to turn it on.

"Ohhh, your gifts are in the house, but you can get them later."

Ashley chimes in. "What time y'all trying to go out?"

"I guess like eleven."

It's time to getting bricks out of that bag; put that scale back on the desk.

Everybody got to rapping along. The ladies were going word for word. These women didn't really do the R&B thing. They liked hood niggas and hood music.

Eron and Sincere made it back quickly, setting the box of liquor and bags down, joining the party. People were well fed. Everybody was mingling, and drinks were flowing. Everybody was good. It was a gathering that people didn't want to end, but everybody was also ready to separate so that the club could be shut down upon their entrance.

It was time to marry the game, and I said, "Yeah, I do." If you want it, you gotta see it with a clear-eyed view.

Meek Mill would've been proud of the concert that Eron and Aaliyah put on in the car on the way to club. They were still feeling the effects of the dinks at the barbeque, so they were buzzing. Eron shifted the Yukon in and out of the lanes.

Eron turned the music down, causing Aaliyah to look at him like he was crazy. "Bitch, don't kill my vibe."

Eron laughed, "Dog! Who the fuck are you talking to? You know what? That smart-ass mouth is going to keep you from getting your gifts."

Aaliyah's eyes damn near bulged out of her head. "I'm sorry."

"Nah, fuck that! You good!"

"Come on. I'll suck yo' dick!" Aaliyah giggled, mimicking the movie *Menace II Society*.

"Don't make me whip this muthafucka out."

"Come on. Please! Give me my gift."

"Quit whining, li'l nigga. It's in the glove box."

Aaliyah damn near ripped the glove compartment to shreds. "Yes, I like little blue boxes." She opened the boxes of a medium Tiffany Somerset toggle bracelet in sterling silver and Tiffany solitaire diamond earrings in platinum.

"Aww, baby. This stuff is beautiful, but you've made my graduation day great. I don't need anything else." Sometimes Aaliyah would get overwhelmed by all the things Eron did for her. Aaliyah appreciated everything he did but didn't want him to feel like he had to.

The thing about Eron was that he didn't want to run Aaliyah's life. He wasn't the type who needed to feel like a man by making sure his woman needed him for every move she made. This was what Aaliyah loved the most about Eron. He never attempted to hinder her and only helped her to be her best. What kind of man do you know who tells his woman to prepare for life without needing a man, including him? That was a real nigga. Nope, that was a real man. The streets helped raise him, but that was Big E's son all day long.

"Aaliyah, what did I tell you about telling me what to do and what not do for my woman? I'll always do and give you what I feel like you deserve. You just graduated college, baby. That shit ain't normal coming from where we come from. You had all the odds against you. You could've taken a different route, but you didn't. Listen, real talk, you don't have to work, but you been working and grinding since I met you. That shit sexy. I get turned on seeing you do homework and shit. You're different. You'll get anything and everything from me."

Aaliyah was left speechless. She didn't even realize that they were pulling up behind Mal's navy blue Charger. Eron watched Aaliyah hurrying up to hop out of the car. Aaliyah smiled because Eron would always cower away after saying something soft. He waited at the front of the car, talking to Dior and Mal as the valet opened the passenger-side door for Aaliyah.

Aaliyah stepped out of the car, looking fierce. Graduation night it's only right that you look the part. She was wearing a white fitted crop top, fitted distressed ripped jeans, and tan Steve Madden booties with studs all over them. She accessorized with a Bella Ecienna body chain that started out as a necklace then fell down between her breasts and wrapped around her waist inside of her belt loops. The body chain could give any outfit life. The outfit was topped off with the graduation cap.

The group walked toward Aaliyah to head into the club.

"Look at you, Ms. Dior!" Dior was looking nothing short of fantastic. Dior wore a tight body con Pepsi blue dress with silver accessorizes and black Christian Loubotins on her feet. Of course, the graduation hat set it off. It was the real star of the show.

"Why thank you. I must admit that you guys make a handsome-looking couple."

Eron was always simple. He wore all black: black Gucci tee, pure black True Religion jeans. On his feet, he wore black Gucci sneakers and the red and green belt with the silver G buckle. Eron rubbed his goatee jokingly. "You know how I do! I'm just trying to look like this rich guy." He looked at Mal.

"Man, here you go, dog." Mal chuckled. "Dog, come on. We got some celebrating to do." Mal was dressed in all white. He wore a polo shirt, True Religion jeans, a Ferragamo belt, and red with white Ferragamo sneakers. In Detroit, niggas always made sure their belt and shoe game was on point.

The outside of the club resembled a car show. Niggas were in everything from foreign whips to old-school Chevy Caprices. That was one thing about Detroit: when you came out into the nightlife, you better pull out the big-boy toys. The line was wrapped around to the side of the building. Detroit nightlife was something for everybody to experience.

"Congratulations to the graduates, y'all!" a voice from the line yelled.

Dior and Aaliyah looked back, not knowing at first who said it, but they quickly spotted a woman who clearly had been drinking waving her arms in the air. Nonetheless, a compliment was a compliment, and it was well appreciated.

"Thank you!"

"Thanks!" Dior chuckled. "Shit we need to get like her."

The group made their way into the club. Eron and Mal slapped fives with the bouncers, heading straight to the VIP section of the club. The club was doing numbers. It was always packed though. Shoulder to shoulder. It was the type of crowd that would be unbearable if you didn't have a booth in VIP. You probably wouldn't have a good time otherwise. Apparently, the general admission club-goers didn't think so. It was turnt all the way up! The knob was broke.

Mal contacted one of the hottest hosts from Detroit, Rob. Rob was always entertaining the crowd. He cracked jokes. He was definitely good at what he did.

"Uh-oh. My niggas Mal and E just walked in the building. Shit about to get real. What up, doe?"

The DJ mixed in Meek Mills' lyrics: *Now there's a lot of bad bitches in the building (Amen). A couple real niggas in the building (Amen).*

Rob continued, "And they didn't come by themselves tonight. They got their baddies with them. College graduate baddies, too! One time for the college girls! Congratulations, beautiful ladies."

"Ayyyyyyye," Dior said, doing a little booty shake.

Aaliyah saluted the host of the event as she did a little slow wind.

"This one is for my college girls!" Rob yelled, prompting the DJ to play the hit "Scholarships" by rapper Juicy J.

They finally made it to their booth to find Ashley, Sincere, and A.J chilling with drinks flowing. Eron and Mal both cringed at the sight of A.J. but for two different reasons. Eron cringed because he never liked the nigga A.J. There was no trust there. He did good business though. Business trumped personal feelings for now.

Mal was irritated because he didn't want Dior feeling uncomfortable in any shape, form, or fashion. She was going to have a good time with him and his people.

"I wasn't sure what y'all were drinking, so I got a bottle of Patrón and Rémy Martin."

"That's a start! I need my graduates to catch up," Eron said.

Meanwhile, Dior felt A.J. staring at her. Mal watched the exchange. "What up, A.J.?" Mal asked, tired of the nigga being a creep.

"Ain't shit. Are we having recap of the other day or something?"

"Nah, it's a wrap on that," Mal said, taking a shot and turning the other way. A.J. was looking dumber than usual. The energy was good. After a couple shots, everybody was on their feet vibing to the music and with each other.

"Another shot. One time for me and my new friend Dior on completing such an irritating task. And shout out to the amazing people who made sure the knob was broke all day."

"Ayyyyyyeeee," the group cheered.

Rob was on the mic, acting a damn fool and talking about all kind of shit. "Aye, but, DJ, I heard the college girls want some T.I. What you got for them?"

T.I.'s "Whatever You Like" came on.

Rob busted through the music. "Nah. Nah, they ain't ready! What else you got for them, Mr. DJ?"

The DJ changed the music, and people were walking around mean mugging. That's just what T.I.'s classic hit "Motivation" did to you. It put you in a zone.

"Shot!" Dior yelled, handing everybody shots.

A.J. thought he was being incognito about the confusion and dislike for Dior being there and not with him. A.J. was really mad at the fact that he been trying to get close to Mal and Eron forever. A.J. knew that Eron never cared for him. That was no secret. A.J. figured that he would work on trying to be Mal's right-hand man. That would never happen. Dumbass A.J. showed how dumb he really was by thinking he had a chance.

Sincere tapped Mal and Eron. "This nigga is going to be a problem."

"I been telling this nigga that, bro. And the nigga took his bitch? Oh yeah, he hot about that."

Mal laughed even though they knew this wasn't a situation that should be taken lightly. "Shit, this ain't what he really want. Man, he better take a different route."

"Straight up!" Sincere and Mal slapped fives while Eron balled his face up, shaking his head.

"Most definitely. Y'all ready to go?" Eron asked without waiting for an answer. By the time they made it back over to the booth, the ladies were taking another shot.

"Damn, cuz! I didn't know y'all was coming here tonight. I would've just rode with y'all." Eron turned around to his ratchet-ass cousin Tierra's voice. He was shocked at who was standing next to Tierra.

"What, dog, you knew we were coming here?"

Tierra laughed. "Maybe I did. Hey, Aaliyah, and what's your name? Dior."

Dior laughed. "Oh, you know my name."

Aaliyah ignored the greeting, looking dead at Jessica. "So you're Jessica, huh?" Aaliyah had never really seen Jessica. The young girl had been talking shit via Instagram and Facebook forever. Aaliyah just never fed into it. Aaliyah looked the girl up and down. She could see why Eron didn't take the kid seriously. The girl was the club in street clothes. Aaliyah had nothing against gym shoes, but Lebron's shouldn't have been a part of any chick's attire who was in Club LAX. Jessica wore Detroit's own "Jo's Coney Island" tee and jeans. The bitch wasn't seeing

Aaliyah. Point blank period. The proof was written all on Jessica's face. She appeared to be uncomfortable and sneaky.

If looks could kill, Jessica and Tierra would be dead, Eron's cousin or not.

"Aye, cuz, we were just heading out." Eron's tone was even, but the look on his face was deadly. It scared the shit out of Tierra. She held a knowing look. Tierra knew that she may be meeting the person she thought she was exempt from meeting: Street Eron, the monster. She grabbed Jessica's hand and couldn't get out of the club fast enough.

Sincere ushered the group through the crowded club. He knew somebody was about to feel Eron's fire. Niggas weren't going to like it. They were going to feel it.

Eron whispered in Aaliyah's ear, "Go to the car, and let me go to the bathroom." He could feel Aaliyah tense up.

Yup. She's pissed.

Mal, Sincere, Ashley, and Dior all walked out of the club. The valet brought up all the cars but Eron's. Aaliyah was beyond pissed and just wanted to get in the car. Nobody wanted to say anything to Aaliyah. The look on her face said, "I don't want to be bothered."

Aaliyah marched over to the valet. "Just give me my car keys. I can cross the street and get it."

"Are you sure, ma'am?"

"Jay, man, just give her the keys. Thanks. And we are going to have a talk about promptness. Especially when it comes to taking care of my family."

"Yes, sir," Jay, the valet, replied, handing over the keys.

Aaliyah snatched the keys. "All right, bro. Bye, y'all."

"Be safe," came from Ashley and Sincere.

"I'ma get your number from Mal to call and check on you tomorrow."

"All right, cool," Aaliyah replied with sad eyes. She wasn't even sad, just pissed that Jessica felt that it was okay to approach her. And what the fuck was Eron doing or saying to the bitch that would make her want to make herself seen?

Aaliyah shrugged her shoulders, looking both ways before crossing the street. Aaliyah made it to the two yellow lines that split the streets. She looked both ways and proceeded to cross the street.

"Car!" a person outside the club yelled just as Aaliyah was picked up by the car. Aaliyah lay on the bumper of the car until the end of the block when she fell off the truck. Upon impact, Aaliyah felt her teeth rip from her gums. Aaliyah was able to glance at the driver, who laughed wickedly. The truck sped off. Aaliyah slid up the street, scratching her whole body against the pavement. She was left lying in the middle of the street, hearing people screaming for someone to call for help.

Am I okay? Did I die? What did I do wrong? Did I look both ways? Aaliyah's mind ran rampant.

"Aaliyah!"

"Oh my God!"

"Baby, it's going to be all right!" Eron, Mal, Dior, Sincere, and Ashley made it down the block in record speed. Eron immediately fell to the ground with tears in his eyes.

Aaliyah glanced at Mal and Dior standing off to the side with a surprised look on their faces.

"The EMTs are on their way," someone from the crowd hollered.

"Eron, did I do something wrong?"

It broke Eron's heart even more for Aaliyah to ask what she could have done differently. "Nothing, baby! They were just being reckless and probably drunk."

"I'm scared. I can't feel my legs. What's wrong with them?"

"I don't think—"

Aaliyah cut him off as his tears met the tears on her face. "Don't play me. Be honest."

"Aaliyah, shit. I don't know. They are going the wrong way."

Aaliyah cried even harder. "I'm twenty-two with broken legs. What am I going to do? Maybe I shouldn't have gone and got the car myself."

"Come on now. Stop it. You're going to be okay. I promise the person who did this will not live let alone walk. I mean that." Eron meant every word. "Somebody call the EMTs again. I don't want her just lying in the street."

Dior yelled through tears, "I just called back. They just keep saying that they're on the way."

Flashing lights could be seen in the distance, and sirens could be heard. It was the police coming to do crowd control. The cops got out of the car. "Sir, please don't attempt to move the body."

Eron looked at the young cops like they were crazy. "I'm not going to move her, but I'm not about to let my girl lie out here in the street without me near."

"Sir, we are just making sure."

Mal walked out into the street to give Eron some comfort. The last thing he needed was to be in jail.

"Ma'am, the EMTs are near. We need for you to keep talking. Can you do that? You're going to be fine."

Mal just wasn't feeling the cops, so he jumped in, sitting on the ground and rubbing Eron's back. "Sis, man, you gon' be all right."

"Man, Mal, don't come over here being soft," Aaliyah said, amazing everybody as she giggled.

"Man, Aaliyah, you are crazy."

Eron was a mess watching the exchange. He felt horrible that he wasn't there to protect her. "Did y'all call Mama and my auntie?"

"No, we haven't called them yet."

"Aaww, man, don't call them. They are going to blow it all out of proportion," said Aaliyah.

"Babe, we have to tell them," Eron replied. "Sin, call Mama and Auntie Jackie. Tell them that we're going to St. John Hospital since it's the closest."

Just as Eron finished his statement, the EMTs pulled up.

"All right, baby. They are here."

"Please. Don't leave me."

"Baby, I'm not. I promise."

"Hi, sir," the paramedic greeted Eron. Eron couldn't speak even if he wanted to. He was in a zombie state as he stepped back out of their way.

"Ma'am, we're going to get you to the hospital. Can you tell me your full name?"

Aaliyah's adrenaline had been pumping earlier, so she wasn't feeling much pain, but now she was coming down from the adrenaline high. She was in pain. "Aaliyah Marie Banks."

"Okay good. Stay with me. How old are you?"

"Twenty-two."

"Okay. We're going to place you on the stretcher."

Aaliyah busted out in a heaving cry. It was heartbreaking for everybody to watch from the sidelines. "No. No. Please don't move me. It's going to hurt."

"Ma'am, we have to get you to the hospital. It will be quick, I promise. Count with me. One, two, three."

"Ahhhh." The paramedics lifted Aaliyah, and she let out a bloodcurdling scream. Aaliyah cried and cried. Her family watched on helplessly, wishing they could help alleviate her pain.

"Eron, ride with me."

"I'm right here. Y'all meet us there." Everybody ran to their cars.

The ride to the hospital was painful for both Aaliyah and Eron. Aaliyah was feeling every bit of the accident. Eron was upset because he couldn't stop her from hurting. It was the longest ride ever. Finally, they pulled up to the hospital entrance, and Aaliyah started to go in and out of consciousness.

"Damn."

"That's crazy."

I was met by so many different emotions. So many feelings were pouring out from the group, even from the boy who gave me such a hard time.

"But what happened after that?"

"Two broken femurs, fractured face, fractured pelvis, nerve damage. I have two rods that my femur bones have grown around." I turned toward the guy who had just given me such a hard time, lifting up right Pink jogging pants leg.

"My scars may not be as visible as yours, hers, or his."

I showed him the long scar that covered both sides of my leg, mimicking a two-sided coin. I took off that same shoe, tapping the heel of my foot and showing how my foot sat straight up with my toes hanging.

"I have no movement in my foot. During the forty-seven days I spent in the hospital, I developed foot drop."

Dropping my pants leg and standing straight up, I pulled the front of my pants down, and everybody gasped. I rolled my eyes because in that moment I didn't give a fuck.

"These incisions right by my crotch are where the doctors put the rods in." The band of my pants snapped against my waist.

"This is a bed sore that goes from one side of my body to the other." Turning around to face them again, I lifted my shirt, just revealing my stomach. "This is where the doctors pulled out the feeding tube." I pointed to the center of my stomach. "This is the mark the tracheotomy left." I wiped every tear that fell because I was angry.

"Here it is years later, and I probably won't ever be able to wear a pair of heels again. Hell, even gym shoes can be uncomfortable. Purses aren't even the same for me. I have to wear a cross-body style or fanny pack so that it's more secure. Therapy will always be a part of my life. And I mean physical and mental therapy. I have a question. Somebody asked me what it felt like to be young and old at the same time."

"Yeah, right."

"No, they did not."

"Yes. Initially, me and this person got into it. I felt that it was an insensitive thing to say. But you know what? It made me think, I am young in age but going through the same things as if I'm old. From wheelchairs to walkers to canes, I have experienced all types of leg and foot braces. I've even learned from an older person to wear my keys around my neck since my balance is not that good. And that's just a piece of my story."

I made no eye contact with anybody as I stopped talking. I was rambling, and I knew it. Some of these feelings I kept buried. So it was a relief getting some of these thoughts out in a room full of like-minded individuals.

"Okay. I think this is a good place to close. But I will say this: God gives His toughest battles to his strongest soldiers. My goal is to get all of our mental capacity to its fullest potential. Do you realize the amount of strength that you all embody? I'm in a room full of fuckin' Transformers!"

Dr. Jenn caused the whole room to bust out laughing. "See y'all next week. If anybody needs anything before then, feel free to contact me. Not all of my patients have my personal cell phone number. But you all do."

Chapter Sixteen

Tineya

It had been weeks since I'd heard Aaliyah's story, and I was still blown away. I was so busy thinking that my situation was so bad that I didn't think about people who had similar situations.

After that session, Aaliyah and I kicked it for a minute. She was cool, and we'd been hanging ever sense. Being around her and her being around me had proven to be therapeutic for us both. She was everything I wasn't. She was strong by nature. She was going with me to handle a situation. She didn't judge me.

Knock. Knock.

I rolled my eyes because whoever knocked at the door was unannounced. Today was a little bit different because I didn't want any influences or opinions on what I felt I needed to do.

"What?" I yanked the door open.

"Damn. What the fuck is up?"

"Nothing. Why are you popping up at my house, Dro?"

"What you mean?" He was stuttering, really looking confused, like he just knew things would be okay.

"Dro, listen. I'm not about to play this game with you. I got something to do so I'ma make this short and sweet. You stood me up. You're a manipulating-ass nigga. You're into me as long as nobody else knows just how much you're into me. You stood me up to ensure that I would stay in the house."

"But—"

"Nah, let me finish. You then come over here with a made-up-ass gift since your 'friend' found what, I'm assuming, was originally meant for me. You allowed this girl to put on a charm bracelet with intricate parts of our relationship on her wrist. Then you took the bitch out that same night that you stood me up. Sounds to me like that's where you'd rather be."

"Man, Tineya, I fucked up. I'm sorry. Let me make it up to you."

I could only laugh at myself for thinking this was the only man I could get. Maybe I was meant to be alone. I didn't know, but I did know I wouldn't settle for what Dro was attempting to give me. I'd be glad when this last piece to the puzzle was over.

"Not to mention you don't like me. Not all of me anyway. You would rather people knowing that you fuck with me but don't fuck with me. You sold dreams, and my dumb ass was buying. But not anymore."

"Tineya, just listen for a minute," Dro reached out, grabbing me by my crossed arms. I stood firm in my stance. We were still in the foyer of my apartment. Dro pushed. "Can you let me in? Damn. Now I get it. I been moving in a fucked-up way. I want you. I always do. I always will. The shit you got is amazing. Best shit I've ever had. Why are you fucking up our shit?"

Is this nigga serious? I blanked out for a minute. I couldn't believe the candidness of this nigga. But it was my fault for allowing his bullshit to stand on a real nigga's ground. I was so hung up on the way we met that I allowed him to treat me mediocre as hell. He really did the bare minimum, and I was okay with that just because of this scar.

"Did you hear me, Tineya?"

Let me try this. "Listen, Dro. Just listen for a minute. In a perfect world, how would you want me? Where do I score in your life?"

"Why do we have to define shit? We been doing good."

"Enough said." I could only push my bottom lip forward and out.

"T—"

Knock. Knock.

"Who the fuck is that?" Dro asked, looking at me with death in his eyes.

The gall of this nigga. "Look, Dro, I gotta go. I have an appointment to get to. It was fun while it lasted. There is no bad blood on my end. You just ain't for me and I ain't for you." I said with a shrug of the shoulders. I yanked the door open.

"Well hello to you." Aaliyah stepped in, looking a fucking model. She looked from Dro to me. "Is everything all right?"

"What the fuck you mean is everything all right?" Dro wore an irritated expression. "And who the fuck are you?" Dro pointed his index finger toward Aaliyah. I smacked my hand on my forehead.

"I'm nobody." Aaliyah snickered in a cool voice, sticking her hand in her purse. "But you should watch how you talk to nobody. Tineya, you ready?"

"Yeah, I'm ready. Come on, Dro, I gotta go." I pulled Dro toward the door, locking my apartment up.

"You really gon' do this in front of her?"

I kept right on walking in the direction of Aaliyah's blacked-out Yukon Denali. Dro smacked his lips, stomping off to his car. I leaned back, letting the tears fall. The entire ride Aaliyah said nothing until we made it to our destination.

"Aye, you know you don't have to do this if you don't want to. You know that, right?"

I wiped a tear, looking at the sign on the building. "You know I ain't gon' lie. I never thought the first time I got pregnant I'd even fucking consider getting an abortion. But I'd be miserable and stupid to bring a child into this situation. My mind is made up."

We got out of the car, walking into the abortion clinic. I wasn't sure about a lot of things, but one thing I knew was that I wouldn't be leaving the same way I came.

Chapter Seventeen

Aaliyah

I'm an asshole. I been like that before I had dough.

Detroit's own "Off Rip" blared through the speakers as Aaliyah and Eron were let into the strip club.

Do what the fuck I want to. Got these niggas mad, but what the fuck they gon' do?

Eron couldn't help but rap along as he made his way through the strip club. Eron ushered Aaliyah into a booth toward the back of the club so that they could keep an eye on the door and have a view of the whole club. Niggas was always hating, so they'd rather be safe than sorry.

"Baby, you good?"

"Yeah, I'm good."

Eron was dressed simply. He wore a black polo V-neck shirt that gripped his muscles yet hung loosely on the abs. He had on black True Religion jeans with plain horseshoes on the pockets. He wore all-black Christian Lobs on his feet.

"Be right back."

"Aye, where are you going?"

Aaliyah laughed. "Can I go the bathroom, daddy? Damn!"

"You need me to go with you?"

"I think I can handle it," Aaliyah replied, smirking as she stood up to go to the bathroom. She made it to the front of the booth and looked back at Eron. She knew when it came to her Eron couldn't hide his desire.

It'd been a couple years. She was happy that she still had his attention. As she made her way through the club, she knew that he was watching. Aaliyah had a mean body. She didn't have to do much to be seen. She was pretty as could be and curvy as the letter S. On this day she wore a white cropped, fitted top around her thirty-six-inch bust, leaving her stomach out on display. Eron kept her in the gym. Oh, the waistline was sick, going into a measly twenty-four inches. On Aaliyah's forty-two-inch ass she wore skinny white True Religion jeans that fell on her navy blue and white high-top Maison Margiela sneakers.

Aaliyah made her way through the club with envious looks from females and looks of want from men. Aaliyah didn't have beauty created from a magazine. She was a real-life beauty. Her brown skin wasn't blemish-free, but her beauty shined through. After using the facilities, she headed back to the booth just in time to see Eron getting drinks and singles from the waitress. She knew this night would be long.

As soon as she sat down, Eron grabbed her, pulling her close. "You kill shit, and you don't even know it! You do the shit so effortlessly. You know that shit turns me on." Eron continued to talk into the back of her neck, causing her breaths to get deeper and labored. "You don't even have on a heel and you fucking over these bum-ass bitches. See, that's why you my bitch!" Eron couldn't even get it out before he was laughing and Aaliyah was punching him in the arm. Their situation was weird like that. No official titles were given, but they operated as a couple. Eron was a man who operated off of instincts. He felt that Aaliyah was good and genuine, and he wanted her around him.

"All right, all right, enough with this soft shit." Aaliyah laughed, standing up as the DJ began playing the classic T.I. strip club anthem "Get Loose."

Eron waved several big-booty strippers over to their table. He loved when they could just let loose. The girls were over there in a matter of seconds. Aaliyah scooted close to Eron toward the middle of the booth, allowing the strippers to dance all around the table. Eron pulled out five hundred-dollar bundles, pushing some over to Aaliyah. Aaliyah took the money, and they together began raining money all over the strippers. Aaliyah slyly slid the waitress five hundred-dollar bills to bring change. The waitress brought the money back, and Aaliyah set it on the table.

Eron looked at Aaliyah with more desire than ever. That's why he chose Aaliyah. Aaliyah was one of a kind!

"Let's go!" Eron said in his deep voice. Aaliyah didn't ask any questions as she got up, following his lead. They left the strippers confused but happy at all the money that was left on the table.

"Um, excuse me! You leaving something, ain't you?" one of the honest strippers yelled over the music. There was no way Eron could've heard her, but Aaliyah did.

"Nah, baby, y'all have a good night," Aaliyah said as Eron guided her through the club. The stripper was stuck.

As they made it outside, the valet was pulling Aaliyah's black Impala to the door.

"Will you drive?" Aaliyah asked, really more like begged Eron to drive. He hated to drive.

"Man, what?" Eron replied.

"Please."

Eron snatched the keys. Hopping in the car, they cruised down Eight Mile to their Livonia house.

"Unzip them jeans for me."

Eron wasn't surprised. Since the first time they had sex, he unleashed the freak. She wanted it all the time, no matter the place. He taught her that what she wouldn't do, the next female would. Aaliyah showed him every chance she got that she wanted her spot.

Eron unbuckled and unzipped his pants, releasing his grown-man-sized dick. Aaliyah looked at his dick with hunger. She appreciated his dick and all the damage that it could administer. Her mouth began to water as she leaned over to take him into her mouth. She slowly licked all around the head of his dick.

"Um." A deep grunt escaped Eron's mouth.

Aaliyah began to bob up and down on his penis. She began to use her right hand to jack his dick off. Aaliyah worked her mouth like no other. The head was always sloppy. If it wasn't sloppy, then it wasn't right.

Gargle. Gargle. It always sounded like she was gargling mouthwash. She was the dick pleaser rapper Lil Wayne rapped about. She went to almost any extreme to make Eron happy.

"Fuck, girl. Suck that shit." It took all of Eron's concentration to pull into the driveway. He yanked her head up, bringing her lips to his lips. "Stop trying to make me cum. You know how I like to cum. Now get the fuck out of the car and take that shit off while you doing that."

Aaliyah eagerly hopped out of the car, pulling her cropped top over her breasts and pulling her jeans off completely. Eron made it around to her side of the car in epic speed. He dropped his pants to his ankles, stepping out of them completely and kicking them to the side. Aaliyah just looked on; she loved when he turned into an animal stalking its prey. His eyes would turn dark and get low. His voice would get even raspier. His tongue would damn near be on the floor. This was usually when she backed down and let him take the lead. He pushed her up against the car roughly yet tenderly, kissing her mouth with so much passion. Eron was a smart dude. He knew what women wanted, and he never wanted their sex life to become routine or robotic. He took the time to learn Aaliyah's body specifically.

"Mmm."

"Umm." They collectively moaned together.

Eron then used his thick, wet tongue to kiss that spot on Aaliyah's left side of her neck that made her weak every time.

"Shit!"

"That's what I like to hear, baby. Talk to me then. Tell Eron what you want me to do. You know it do something to me every time you say my name. Nobody can say it like you do."

"Baby, I want you to eat my pussy."

Eron sat her on top of the hood of the car, diving in head first. "That's the shit I like to hear."

"Shit!"

As soon as Eron's soft, wet tongue made contact with Aaliyah's pussy, it got even wetter, and she lost it. Eron would lay his tongue flat up against her clit and close his lips around it, pulling it lightly. Eron was a master at the art of eating pussy. He always used the right amount of pressure. He took the time to pay attention to what made her body weak.

"Shit. Right there. Don't move. I'm about to cum."

When Aaliyah said stuff like that, Eron wasn't like most men. He actually listened. He stayed there, and before they knew it, he was drinking up every drop of Aaliyah's love fluids.

"Damn I love you!" Aaliyah couldn't help but declare.

"Man, get the fuck on with that soft shit and turn over."

Aaliyah just laughed because they both had times when they be trying to act hard. They were both butter to each other through and through, and it was no secret.

"I hear you, nigga," Aaliyah replied, following the instructions that were given.

Aaliyah was always ready to show out. She pushed Eron up against their house, then she turned around, grabbing her ankles. Aaliyah knew that Eron liked to watch her ass. He took in the beauty before his eyes as he walked toward his prize, rubbing his dick on the way. Eron took his dick and began grinding up and down Aaliyah's pussy.

"Um," Aaliyah moaned.

Eron felt Aaliyah's knees buckle as he ran his fingers through her Remy weave that he loved so much. He then suddenly yanked her head back, kissing her mouth with so much urgency.

"Ohhh, I love this dick," Aaliyah moaned. It was close to being inaudible, but Eron knew his bitch.

"I know you do. You ain't gon' get this shit anywhere else. Remember that!" Eron knew that Aaliyah only had eyes for him, but he knew that he wasn't living right. He knew that niggas would pay for a bitch like Aaliyah's time. He wasn't naïve to that fact.

He used his dick, rubbing it from the clit to her vagina. He pushed his dick in, and as always it was struggle. Aaliyah had the true definition of that "snap back." He loved it.

"Shit, Aaliyah! Damn!"

"Ummm put it all the way in! Stop playing with me!"

Eron always had to take his time going in for the first time because Aaliyah was always wet, warm, and so inviting. He rocked back and forth at a slow pace for a while.

"Um. Um. Stop playing and fuck me," Aaliyah moaned. Eron heard her loud and clear and started beating the pussy out the frame.

"Shit. I'm close. Don't stop." Aaliyah was a minute woman with Eron. He knew just how to hit it. Aaliyah could stop and start over again all night.

Eron was in tune with her body. He knew that she was close. He was close too. The combination of her hot love canal, seeing the waves her booty was making, and hearing her moan, he was so close. He would never come first though. He wasn't that type of nigga. Aaliyah knew this.

"I'm cumming."

"Oh shit, I'm cumming with you."

Eron put all of his kids in Aaliyah just as always. They sat on the side of their house breathing hard for fifteen minutes until Eron carried Aaliyah into the house.

"I love you, girl."

"I love you too," Aaliyah replied breathlessly into his ear.

"Wake yo' ass up," Eron yelled in my ear. "What the fuck you dreaming about that had that muthafucka hot and ready? You want me to fuck you up?"

I popped my eyes open. I was staring at a frowned-up Eron.

"What you talking about? You know, yo' ass can fuck up a wet dream."

Eron flexed his jaw. It turned me on in so many ways. Hell, I was already horny from that damn dream. He stood in front of me all angry wearing some basketball shorts, no shirt, and ankle socks. I could see that he'd been working out. Ever since we'd moved from Livonia back to Indian Village on Detroit's east side, he'd been working out even more. The 240 pounds he was when I met him was now about 260 pounds. He wasn't all hard body, but I appreciated the extra weight.

"I was thinking about that one time we went to that strip club."

"We always in somebody strip club. Be more specific."

"This is true," I said with laughter. "But one of the first times we hung out together."

"Oh, when that car ride got real?"

"Yeah."

Eron stood at the side of the bed while I lay in the bed. Instantly, both of us looked toward my phone to see what time it was.

"We got a little time."

"Okay."

Our lips crashed into each other. He started to pull my shirt over my head while I snatched his shorts down.

"Just let me suck it."

"Go ahead," he said with a grunt.

He sat on the bed with his legs hanging off the bed. I sat up on my knees with my mouth watering. I thought about giving him head while just leaning over, but he loved when I was on my knees in front of him. Using a decorative pillow from the bed, placing it on the floor as a cushion, I grabbed ahold of his dick.

While looking him directly in his eyes, I took one long lick from the bottom to the tip of his dick, only stopping to pay close attention to the V-shaped part under the head of his dick where the glans meets his thick, long-ass shaft.

"Sss." I watched as Eron gripped the sheets, lifting off the bed. I wrapped my mouth around his dick, allowing it to touch the back of my throat. I did this to gather as much spit as I could. I wanted my mouth as wet as it could get. I went up and down, taking in as much of his dick as I could.

"Guggh!" The sound of me gagging could be heard throughout the room. Don't worry though. He loved that sound.

"Shit, girl!"

I winked. I continued to make the sound. I was going up and down, spinning my head round and round and acting as a suction cup. I knew he was close. I pulled his dick from my mouth with a loud pop. There was a stream of spit hanging from his dick to my mouth.

"Uhh." I used my hand, gripping his dick with just the right amount of strength. From the top to the bottom in a circular motion, I jacked his dick.

"Ahhh." He was always so cool. Sex was the one of the only times he exposed his hand. So this I enjoyed tremendously. Taking my mouth and placing it on the head of his dick, I made a sucking motion. I was only covering the sensitive part below the mushroom head. That move in conjunction with an up-and-down twisting motion and the spit that worked its way down his penis had him in pure bliss.

"Shit." He grabbed my sew-in for dear life.

"Hmmmm." I started to hum, making my throat vibrate.

"I'm about to cum." I tasted his thick semen shoot down my throat. I kept sucking until I slurped him dry.

"Aaliyah! Stop fucking playing." Eron shied away from my touch. His dick popped from my mouth just like it did earlier but with finality.

Chapter Eighteen

Tineya

I sat at my dining room table, working on an assignment for the closeout of the group therapy session. We were going to write a letter to the person who had done us wrong. The plan was to write it, read it aloud, seal it, and put it in a box. This task had proven to be harder than I thought.

"Finally."

Just as I finished, my phone was ringing. "Hello."

"Dog, tell me you didn't kill my baby!"

"What?" My heart fell into my stomach. Although Dro was the absolute worst, I still didn't want to hurt him. Not the way he hurt me.

"Did you have an abortion?"

"Who told you that?"

"Salena. Damn it, I never thought you would do me like that. But I know it's true 'cause she had no reason to lie."

"Dro. We had no right bringing a baby into the world. Just because we chose to operate in dysfunction didn't mean we should take away an innocent child's right to live in peace."

"Man, fuck all that! You a selfish, rotten, pussy-ass bitch. You know what? I'm happy you killed the bastard. I don't need a baby by yo' deformed ass. Hell, I wouldn't even make you my bitch, so I really didn't need yo' ass as my baby mama."

I listened to the nigga go off on me. I secretly felt guilty about my decision to abort the baby. Not because of Dro though. On one hand, I knew that we didn't need a kid in this fucked-up situation. On the other hand, I felt I didn't reserve the right to use an abortion as a contraceptive.

"You a dumb-ass bitch," Dro grunted. "You was lucky that pussy hit like no other because ain't nobody gon' take you serious. You would be fine, but that ugly scar won't allow you to be bad."

I just held the phone as Dro rambled on and on, calling me everything but a child of God.

As if something snapped in my mind, I could only think about how he knew that the abortion took place. Salena. I didn't want to believe it. It made me think of how distant both Uncle Nathan and Salena had been acting. Since my parents died and I was living on my own, he would religiously keep money in my account for bills and a little to play with. But he hadn't been checking on me or interacting with me at all.

"Tineya. Bitch, you hear me?" I had forgot he was even on the phone.

"Do I hear you? Yes, I hear you. I'm the ugly girl with the scar. Blah. Blah. Blah. You singing the same song. This is why I wouldn't ever bring a kid into the world with you as his father. You just evil. But that's neither here nor there. Fuck you. And have a nice life."

"Bitch, you bet' not hang up. What you mean you wouldn't have a baby with me? So you'll have another nigga's baby?"

I gasped as I hung up the phone. "Fuck this." I felt my body getting hot as I grabbed my keys and the letter for therapy, rushing out the door, fueled by anger.

Taking a deep breath, I headed for Salena's apartment building. The drive was made in half the time. I hoped that Dro's ass was lying. I really wanted to give Salena the benefit of the doubt.

I couldn't stop the tears if I tried. If there was one thing I hated about myself, it was the inability to hide my emotions. Whenever I got worked up, I cried. I took the idiom "wearing your heart on your sleeve" to an all-new height. I expressed my emotions without restriction, without caution, for all to see. To hurt my feelings was an easy task. Sometimes people used it against me.

Knock. Knock.

I felt fear taking over. No, I wasn't scared of Salena, or anybody else for that matter. It was the fear of knowing the truth. It wasn't easy for anybody to feel like somebody they were close to would cross them.

It wasn't long before the locks could be heard clicking, and there stood Salena. Not surprising, she almost looked like she was waiting on somebody.

"He told me you were probably coming here." She smirked as she moved to the side, giving me room to enter the apartment.

"So, you really did tell him?"

"Come on now. You asking questions you already know the answer to," Salena said in the same smug tone that I was used to seeing, just not toward me. It blew me back.

"Damn. Like that huh? Why?"

"Yeah, I told him. I think you was wrong for that. You took his choice away."

"Now you're advocating for him?"

"I mean you just selfish. You think the world revolves around you. I mean shit happened to you, but so what?"

I stepped back, almost as if I were seeing Salena for the first time. The bitch was sitting in the same class with Dro. All this time, they really had been pulling the wool over my eyes.

"I mean shit. You not all that. You went to school. So what? You're about to graduate, and you have no family besides Nathan. Who gon' be there for you? You really need us. You were wrong. Get over it."

I was furious. "You know what? Fuck you." I attempted to leave but was snatched back by Salena.

"Bitch!" I turned around, punching Salena dead in the mouth. The move caught Salena off guard. Hell, it caught me by surprise too, but Salena wouldn't know it.

"You fucking hit me!" Salena said in a tone of disbelief while dramatically holding her cheek.

I hit her again, folding her like a pretzel. I felt some pressure falling off of me with each hit I landed.

"Bitch, get out of my house. I'm calling the police."

I shook my head, never breaking my stride. I mirrored a pit bull the way my breathing was labored. I was so mad as I marched from the apartment. I reached back, shutting Salena's door. Only my ass would fight somebody and make sure I shut their door behind me.

My feelings were in an uproar. As I pulled out of the complex, I cried. Frustration seeped through my pores.

Ring. Ring. Ring. Aaliyah called and called. I was late for the group therapy session.

Damn. Twenty minutes! Can this day get any worse?

Chapter Nineteen

Aaliyah

"Wow," Dr. Jennifer expressed just as Tineya slid into the back of the room. "These letters are powerful. I just want you guys to get out all of these ill-will emotions. The definition of resentment is a feeling of displeasure at having been treated unfairly. Sound familiar? This is your life, not the life of the person who wronged you! The beauty of this thing called life is that since you only get one you're forced to live it! Now, we have two more letters to read."

Aaliyah stuck her church finger up in an interruption. Come on now, I know you know what a church finger is. You know, the finger that the members put up if they have to excuse themselves during the church service.

"Yes, Aaliyah?"

"Can you please wait? I know Tineya is coming. I really . . . well, me and Dior—"

"I'm here," Tineya announced with a damp face. It was evident to the room that something had happened. There was something else that stood out, but not even Tineya noticed.

"What's wrong?" Aaliyah asked immediately.

"Nothing. I'm here. Dr. Jenn, you can continue. I'm sorry to interrupt."

Dr. Jenn looked at Tineya. "Are you sure?"

"Yes." Tineya clenched her teeth.

"Okay, Dior, you have the floor. You are the latest member of this group. Your story is way too common."

"Okay." Dior took a breath with her head down.

"You got this," Aaliyah encouraged her. Since she'd known Dior, she'd never seen her second-guess herself. She'd always worn her confidence on her sleeve like a badge of honor. And rightfully so. But anything she'd done she'd stood on.

"Man, I have never put my head down about anything. So, I won't start today."

Dear my brother Drew,

Where do I start? You are the reason I am the way I am. You were the perfect brother. We grew up close. You protected me from everything and everybody. The five years between us, I always thought it was a good thing. The five years would allow you to be a teacher to me.

A teacher is sort of a leadership role. It's usually a positive role though. But you? You were everything but positive. You allowed one "drunken" night change the dynamics of our relationship.

I was nine, and you were fourteen. You wanted to play a game. You wanted to play follow the leader. You were my brother, so I'm thinking that it was okay. You took something I could never get back. Now you're in prison, where you were only sentenced to fifteen years. That's it, when you were the reason our parents lost a son to the system and a daughter to promiscuity. I became this person who didn't care. Since I'm grown now, I can no longer blame you about my adult decisions. I don't want to. But I realized I have a problem. The ability to please a man, eliminating love from the equation, would allow me to never hurt. While I don't regret

*the decisions I made, I still want one man and a
family. I have yet to forgive you, but I am working
toward it to become a better me.*

*Dior looked up for the first time since she opened
the letter. "How did I do?" she quizzed, causing a
chuckle from the group.*

"You stupid." Aaliyah shook her head with a smack to
her forehead. It was all in fun. Dior had the ability to add
some comic relief. She always found a joke in something.
She was obviously deflecting.

"You know, Dior, your spirit is infectious. First, let me
go back. When Aaliyah first told her story, she drifted off
into yours, and I was shocked. Like everybody else in the
room, I wondered why she was telling your business."

Everybody laughed. Aaliyah put her head down.

"Oh no! Y'all know now she ain't tell y'all nothing I
woudn't say. Hell, I got some pictures in my phone if
y'all want to see." Dior's crazy ass started to reach for her
phone.

"No, that will not be necessary."

"Shhhhhhiiiiddd! This one eye work. Y'all got a nigga
crying from his one good eye. Hell, make my rainy days
sunny!" the guy said quickly. When he was three years
old, his mother let who she thought was a good babysitter
watch her son. The young girl had her boyfriend over,
neglecting her job totally. The kid ended up getting run
over by his neighbor. He was left with a permanent black
eye that almost looked as if his eye were melting.

"No! That won't be necessary," Dr. Jenn hurriedly
countered with both hands in a stop gesture.

"Well, I was serious. Let me see."

"Shit, me too."

Dior leaned over, showing the guy a picture in her
phone.

"Damn!"

"I know, right," Dior cockily said, flipping her hair dramatically.

"Anyway . . . Damn. You made me forget what I was going to say," Dr. Jenn went on. "I can't believe you really just showed him a picture. But this is what makes you guys awesome. Y'all could joke about anything anytime. This is admirable. Come on, Aaliyah, you're up."

With a real eye roll, Aaliyah stood up. "This will be short and sweet."

> *Dear the Green Explorer,*
> *I'll never understand how my life turned from sugar to shit in a matter of minutes. You took an important, positive date and made it a negative situation. That day will never be the day I graduated. It will always be the day I got hit by the car. I was so embarrassed, lying on the ground as if I were a science experiment.*
> *I keep wondering what I could've done differently. If maybe I didn't go out, would things be different? How does it feel to be old and young at the same time? I know. My body will never be the same. Physical therapy will always be a part of my life. The aches and pains will always be there. I have arthritis just like an older person. I shouldn't be experiencing these things for at least forty or fifty more years. The pain I still feel around the clock is excessive. How am I forced to take the medicine that rappers are rapping about? They are taking it for play while my doctors are trying to explain to me the effects of medicine and when you need it versus when you don't. I had to learn to do everything all over again. How could you hit someone with a car and keep going? I was planted to the*

front of your truck carrying me for about a half a block, and when my body fell to the ground, you rolled me over. How could you keep going?

I'm not sure forgetting you will ever be an option, but I do forgive you. Not for you, but for me and the development of my relationships.

"Thanks, Aaliyah. Amazing what you said there. Healing is not about the person who did you wrong. You have to, it is a must to, work through these emotions for you to heal. The goal is to be the best version of you. A reason you're here on planet Earth is to evolve, improve, grow, and become the greatest version of yourself. It's documented that being the best you improves different areas of your life, such as your emotions, spirit, body, mind, occupation, and all relationships. Now, last but not least, Ms. Tineya."

Tineya stood up, pushing her straggling hairs into her messy ponytail. It looked like she had her hair in a wrap originally, and that she finger combed it into a ponytail.

Dear the Robbers,

Nick and Tina were my parents. Are my parents. I still struggle with past tense and present tense when it comes to my parents. You took so many things from me. You took January 21, my parents, and my ability to be beautiful. On my birthday, a day when I should be happy, I never am. I saw everything play out. I was present to see the life leave their bodies. You didn't have to do what you did to me. You broke the very mixing bowl that my mother just used to bake something with love. She put her heart into making that cake for my birthday. You used it to cut a child's face. You told me, "Sorry, little mama, you was just a casualty of war."

You said it as if it were okay. As if I should be okay with that. As if I should have some understanding of your fucked-up logic. Now I'm struggling with my worth. Am I worthy of a man? Or do I have to settle for a piece of one? You know? The one who just wants to have sex with me but doesn't want to take me out. All because of this scar that I have no control over. This scar has been a thorn in my side since I got it. It has made people stop and stare. Innocent children point and shit. The grown people try to figure out what happened. Some even having the gall to ask. This is all when I make the mistake of showing the scar. I'm always attempting to hide the scar as best I can. But that doesn't work all the time.

Anyway, I want to get over this. I am trying to forgive and forget. I am trying to have an air of confidence about myself. I want to demand respect from the opposite sex. I don't want to feel as if I have to settle for somebody else's man or that man's secret. All because of this scar.

Tineya sat down with her tears falling on her hands as she folded her paper.

"I want to applaud you, Tineya. You have made so much progress, and you don't even know it. All of you have. Tineya, this is the first time you've pulled your hair back in all of the weeks we've been here. Did you notice that?"

"No, I didn't," Tineya admitted.

"I know you didn't. I do see that something pissed you off. But it's clear that you don't want to talk about it, and that's fine.

"Now this is our last session. This doesn't mean we all can't come together again. I'll see anybody individually as well. Now that that's out of the way, I want to leave you guys with something. Kind of a summary if you will. A breakdown of us as a whole.

"Scars. Scars are what we all have in common. We all have them. Some of our scars are physical, but all of them are mental. Deep-rooted mental scars. We need to acknowledge, accept, and believe that early childhood fears and events deeply impact us as adults. Rape, hit-and-run accidents, promiscuity, accidents, domestic violence, and the list goes on and on. These things that happened to us way back when shape the way we move around in society. We all want acceptance, but we fear rejection. I read an article once, based on a study, that said our personalities can change depending on our experiences as children. Sometimes, rejection can make us try to be perfect. And we all know that's an impossible goal. If that doesn't sum up this group, I don't know what does."

"You better preach!" Dior yelled out, causing everybody to laugh.

"But y'all don't hear me, though!" Dr. Jenn came back with.

"Man, y'all silly as fuck!" Tineya announced.

"Damn. You cuss?" Aaliyah questioned, mocking in fake surprise.

"Fuck you!" Tineya rolled her eyes, joking.

"Hmmmm. You a cutie. Fat ass, too. Wait, let me call Eron and see if I can bring you home." Aaliyah grabbed at her phone, making the room crack the fuck up.

"Oh my gosh! Shut up, idiot."

"You mad 'cause I'll make you my sister wife. Heyyyyy, sis!"

Even Dr. Jenn was laughing and holding her side. "Okay, y'all. I'm trying to wrap up. I just have a little more to leave you crazy people with."

"Dammmn, Dr. Jenn. Tell a nigga how you really feel." The one guy feigned being hurt.

"Poor, poor choice of words." Dr. Jenn shook her head while everybody else laughed.

"Umm hmm!" The group was giving Dr. Jenn a hard time.

"Ohhhh hush."

"Well, at least we ain't sensitive." Dior winked at Dr. Jenn.

"I'll leave you guys with this: a scar comes from your body trying to repair itself. Scars are a natural part of the body's healing process. The point is the body takes time to heal, and so does your mental!"

Chapter Twenty

Aaliyah

"Can you get the door?" Aaliyah yelled from upstairs in the bedroom.

"Hell nah!" Eron shouted back, making his way to the front door. Aaliyah never gave him a response.

"Who the fuck is it?" Eron yanked the door open, causing Tineya to jump.

"Well hello!"

"What up? What up? Come on in." Eron ushered Tineya to the den. "Aaliyah, yo' homegirl down here!" he hollered. "Okay, Tineya, you know where everything is. Make yourself at home. I'm going back in basement with my brother."

"Okay, thanks." Tineya went in the direction of the kitchen to grab a bottle of water. In the short time they'd all known each other she felt comfortable. Almost as if they were brothers and sisters.

Tineya stood in the kitchen and leaned on the island, taking the newly renovated house. It was a beauty. The kitchen was stainless steel and black themed. All of the appliances were black with stainless finishes. The gray tile floor extended throughout the first level of the house. There were accent colors periodically through the house. The house wasn't overly girly. The house held both a pop of colors that a woman would like with the gray undertones that a man would appreciate. It wasn't a massive colonial-style house. The house was airy with tons of light.

Tineya plopped on the sectional in the living room, closing her eyes as she leaned her head back on the couch.

"Wakey, wakey!"

Aaliyah poked Tineya in the side of her neck. "Wake up! Okay, you not that damn tired!"

Tineya opened her eyes to a wineglass in her face. Dior moved the glass back and forth in her face like in the movie *Friday After Next*.

"Man, y'all play too much!"

"Yeah, yeah, whatever."

Tineya grabbed her wine. "Shit, I needed this."

"I see." Dior lay back on the other end of the couch while Aaliyah sat on the floor with a throw blanket draped over her feet.

"I gave you some time. What happened to you on the last day of therapy?" Aaliyah questioned.

Tineya smacked her lips, pulling her side-parted bangs over her right eye.

"Come on now. You knew this was coming. I know we became friends fast. Even you and Aaliyah are more friends than you and I, but even I was concerned. You seemed out of it. Like you had fucking Mount Rushmore on your shoulders."

"Hold up. Dior, roll this up."

"Nigga, no. I did it last time."

"No, you didn't."

"Yes, I did."

While Dior and Aaliyah went back and forth about who was going to roll their blunt, Tineya snatched the jar of medicinal marijuana, breaking it down. She took her time picking out the few stems and seeds. Tineya was lost in her thoughts as she took the Swisher Sweets blunt wrap from its wrapper. She stuck the entire blunt into her mouth, sucking on it lightly and careful to not soak it completely. She used her fingernail to cut the blunt, dumping the tobacco into the blunt wrapper. The weed replaced the tobacco.

"Sis!"

"Now let a nigga find out you a thug."

Tineya came back from her thoughts with a laugh, fixing her bangs and noticing that Eron stood next to two other guys. Eron was by no means small or anything like it.

"What y'all talking about?"

"We talking about your ass pearling that blunt like you throwing up Taylor Gang or Crip walking through the LBC," Aaliyah joked about Snoop Dogg and Wiz, who everybody knew smoked like chimneys.

Everybody snickered except one of the guys. He stood right by the door as if he was waiting for them to leave. The guy's eyes kept finding Tineya's.

"Sooooo, are you going tell us how you are a weed connoisseur?" Aaliyah asked, clapping her hands together.

"My uncle. It was just us, and even though I don't smoke, he made me learn."

"What you mean made you?"

"I mean . . . not like that. I just mean he taught me."

"Aye, Liyah, we're about to go shoot some moves. See y'all later."

"You not gon' say bye to me?" Mal walked up to Dior, standing directly in front of her.

"Fuck you."

He backed up smoothly. "You know that can always be arranged." Dior simply put her middle finger up.

The men left the living room without another word.

Chapter Twenty-one

Tineya

"What was that?"

"Who, Mal?" Dior asked defensively.

"Why? Didn't you just tell him 'Fuck you, daddy'?"

The ladies laughed. "Now you just making shit up," Dior snapped. "Who called him daddy?"

"We could hear your undertone."

"Whatever. It's complicated." Dior waved her hand.

"So anyway. I haven't been feeling the way that people around me have been moving."

"Always trust your instincts."

"My uncle Nathan is my dad's, Nick's, younger brother. After that shit happened to my parents, I became a recluse. I was withdrawn from everything. School, work, that's it. But anyway I moved with my uncle. He's only a few years older, so he took on a huge responsibility by taking me in. We dodged Detroit Child Protective Services together. We grew close. He was all I fucking had. Everybody knows the day of my birthday is also the anniversary of my parents' deaths. Needless to say, I hate it. But this year Salena, Dro, and Nathan asses acting like they hate me. Nathan just start going off on me, telling me how I need to settle with bullshit I been dealing with for years, all because nobody would want to have a girl with a scar on her face."

"What the fuck?" Dior snapped. Aaliyah sat up with her elbows on her knees with damn near smoke coming from her ears.

"Just go ahead. I seen the bitch Salena. I knew I couldn't vibe with her that one time that I met her," she went on to say as she had her phone in her hand. "This why the bitch posting all these lonely-ass 'friends ain't really friends just some cool-ass niggas' posts."

"No, let me tell you. Remember the day I was late to therapy? We actually got into a fight."

"Stop fucking lying."

"I knew some heavy shit went down."

"So anyway, I confided in her about the abortion, and she told Dro. He went off on me, dragging me through the mud. But when he said it, something in me snapped. I went to her house. The bitch wasn't remorseful at all. She acted as if it were her decision to make. I just hit and kept hitting her. I'm so mad. Like I need another scar." By this time Tineya was pacing.

"Stop worrying about that scar. You cold and you don't even realize it. Fuck them, they toxic. You giving them way too much power over you."

"Way too much. I want to ask you something. You said your dad was a pharmacist, right?"

"Yes."

"That tells me that his shit had to be together. I mean insurance policies and shit like that. I'm thinking that your uncle is in some way benefitting from you."

"What? No. He puts my money in my account like clockwork. He even puts extra in it. I don't think he would move like that."

Dior said, "Man, come on, Tineya. That nigga ain't moving like a real one. He's a snake. A snake in every sense of the word. Slimy and unpredictable. Some foolish people keep a snake as a pet, thinking that if the snake knows them, then it won't turn on its owner. Even if it's the same person who provides its food. Even if it's in a cage and you have it for a long time, a snake is calculating, coming up with a way to get you. A snake doesn't need a reason to attack. It just does it. Long story short, a snake can't be trusted and neither can a human who's moving as suspiciously as your uncle. See, between Jamal and Eron, I am learning people. They always taught Aaliyah ways to read a man. Number one was that a solid person should be able to look another solid person directly in the eyes. I bet Nathan's eyes told a different story from yours. You speak admirably about him, but that's not the person who thinks you should settle.

"An untrustworthy person is always out of touch with reality. Who does that sound like? Sounds like Salena to me. She broke the fucking code. It's some shit that she never should've spoke about if you told her it in confidence. Whether she agreed with moves you was making or not, she should've been riding with you, right or wrong. Period!" Dior finished. "The only people who don't do that want your man or they're jealous. And I am sure the signs were there, but you think the person is all good when all they did was a good gesture. But even then, you have to wonder why they good the good deed. Are they doing it because they will stand to gain?'

Tineya sat there attempting to process the things that were being said. She tried her best to hold on to the one good thing Salena did or how she stood up for her. As fucked up as it sounded, Salena wanted Tineya to suffer at the hands of her and not anybody else.

"This shit actually makes sense."

"The only way to kill a snake is to chop his head off," said Dior.

Chapter Twenty-two

Tineya

"Don't get y'all ass out that car until we get there. And don't park directly in front of the house," Eron said smoothly on speakerphone while they sat in the car just down the block from Tineya's old house. Tineya's palms were sweaty. She'd made it a point to stay away from this house by any means necessary.

"This house still standing it, and it looks good. I'm surprised the crackheads haven't made it through it yet," Dior said absentmindedly.

"Now tell me what happened again. This way, when we get there we can go in with no worries," Eron's voice boomed through the car.

"I think Tineya's father left either money or a policy for her. She remembered that he had a safe. We want to check if anything is in there."

"A snake huh? Does Tineya realize that snakes don't get to live?" Aaliyah looked back at Tineya as she sat wringing her hands as if she wanted to get water from them.

"Wait. Do you mean kill him?"

"Look I'll say this. Snakes plot and scheme until they get what they want. Snakes will lie in the cut until they are ready to attack. That won't happen to me or mine. Get ya head in the game."

Before anyone knew it Eron, Mal, and Ro came back, walking up the street.

"Get out of the car," Eron voiced boomed through the speaker one last time before they heard the line clear.

"Which house?" Ro asked in a raspy, quiet voice. He was dominating. His features were very prevalent even in the dark. His eyes pierced through the dark, looking into Tineya's soul. Tineya pointed in the direction of the house she grew up in. Ro took off in the direction of the house, leaving the group.

"He'll go in first, then he'll come out to get us." About a full minute went by as they stood at the back door. Mal and Eron stood firmly, feet planted just as they show you at a gun range, feet about shoulder-length apart diagonally with the left foot in front of the right foot. They equally blocked the women.

Ro appeared at the door with his finger up to lips in a "Shhhh" motion. They could hear arguing in the basement.

"A.J., I told you I couldn't get nothing out of her."

Everybody looked at each other, listening in a confused fashion.

"Didn't y'all do that bullshit-ass letter-writing shit? Let me see the letter."

"No. No. That's too much. Just too much. I will not allow you to take away the patients' privacy. And why did I have to meet you over here? You could've come to my house like you usually do."

"Are you serious? Now you worried about the privacy shit? You've told me everything y'all discussed thus far. Look, the money is getting low. I need her on the hook. I need her to feel sorry and like she owes me something. I been forging her signature thus far, but now the attorney is requesting to see her."

"I'm sorry. You know I really want to have a baby and be together."

"Well, I need to know what's in those letters. I need to know if the girl knows that I set up that accident. If her boyfriend finds out, I am dead."

"Aaliyah doesn't know. I can assure you. She thinks it was purely her bad luck."

Aaliyah stood back crying silently. She was angry but not as angry as Eron. Mal stood bear-hugging Eron, trying to calm him down so that they could hear what was said.

The first level of the house was pitch-black. They had to thank God that they all wore dark clothes. The steps creaked just as Tineya remembered that they always would. The person who came down the steps didn't even realize a gun was trained on them. The person appeared as if they were waking up from sleep.

"Nathan!"

The person whose voice it was blew Tineya away. It was none other than Salena. She followed the light of the open basement door.

"Who the fuck is that?"

The two voices went back and forth as Salena went down the stairs into the basement.

"Really, Nathan? Really? In the same fucking house?"

"This is my man. Where'd you get her from? He doesn't owe you any explanations."

"Bitch, you don't even know his real name. That's how serious he is about you."

"Okay, y'all, stop. Just stop. We are not getting any-where like this. My bad about y'all finding out like this. But shit, I need y'all both."

Both women stood there crying.

"Jennifer, I needed her to get as much information about how Tineya been feeling. They're best friends."

"Well, we were."

Nathan aka A.J.'s head turned abruptly. "The fuck you mean 'were'? You were supposed to always be my inside source."

Nobody paid attention as Jennifer pulled her registered pistol out of her purse, pointing it at Nathan's back.

Pow! Pow! Pow!

The group looked at each other as a hurt Dr. Jennifer Long walked out the front door frantically.

"Aye, Eron, take Aaliyah out to the car. We gotta move quickly." Ro's gaze shifted to a wide-eyed Tineya.

"The safe is in the basement, right? Okay, either you go down there, or you can give me the combination and I can do it for you, but we gotta be quick."

"Uh . . ." Tineya's hands waved up and down as she tried to think. Ro's gloved hand grabbed her hand in an attempt to bring her back. "I think it's twenty-one, one, nine."

"Okay, go out to the car and wait." Jamal ushered both Tineya and Dior out of the house, wiping down anything along the way. Tineya walked out the door being careful to not touch anything. Only seconds later Ro walked out of the house with a book bag on. Eron hopped in the car. Aaliyah drove because she could barely focus. The car ride was silent. Tineya didn't even notice or care that Ro had the bag with him.

Chapter Twenty-three

Three Months Later

"Please, have a seat at that table second from the last. Don't touch the inmate. She will be coming right out of the double doors," an angry-ass, bad-built correction officer said all in one breath. She didn't bother to wait for a response.

Aaliyah and Tineya looked at each other. "Okay."

They sat as they waited for the person to come out. They couldn't help but feel a wave of sadness wash over them. It was heartbreaking seeing the separation of families. Mothers sitting with their children, trying to explain to them why Mommy couldn't go home or why their contact was limited was tough to see.

"Man, I'm ready to go." No sooner than Tineya said that a very pregnant, miserable-looking Dr. Jennifer Long squealed.

"Oh my gosh! How did you guys know I was here?" She chuckled nervously, looking around at the dreary grayness of the visiting room.

"So you were dating my uncle?"

"We're just cutting right to the chase, huh?"

"Appears that way."

Dr. Jenn slammed her hand on the table. "I did everything right, and now I'm having a baby in prison. I was with a man for years who beat me over and over. He beat me because the meteorologist lied about the *weather. He never needed a reason. I wanted nothing more than a baby. He said he wanted one too. Yet, he beat the mutherfucker out of me.*

"I'd finally had enough. I left him. I went to get my mind right. I went to school. I figured since I couldn't fix myself, I would work on other people's minds. I stayed away from dating. I just didn't need it. But I met A.J., and he swept me off my feet. I didn't expect him to want to know all about my business, but I grew to appreciate it. He told me that he loved me. Then everything started out with, 'If you loved me, then you'd do x, y, and z.'"

"So basically you got manipulated?" Aaliyah questioned.

"See, now you getting it. He asked, and I delivered. I figured if I did what he wanted, we could run away and be happy. It was no coincidence that either of you were assigned to me."

"Now you starting to sound as if you are proud of this shit," Tineya said.

"Oh, look at you. You look confident. Even letting that scar breathe some."

"Jennifer. Jennifer. Jennifer."

Jennifer stood at the small creases of the window, coming back from her daydream. It was a recurring daydream. Each day it got further and further away.

"Jennifer, you have to participate in the group."

She looked around at the small group and couldn't help but compare it to when she ran her own group. "Tiffany." Jennifer started walking toward the empty chair.

"Tiffany? My name is Dr. Daniels. I'd like to be addressed as such."

"Well, you don't call me Dr. Jenn."

Dr. Daniels stood up. "Listen, I don't call you Dr. Jennifer because the fact remains you are not a doctor. You threw that away on a man. You violated a patient-therapist confidentiality clause. I am trying my best to work with you, but you need to understand that I run this session. Whether or not you like the way I run it doesn't matter. You lost that privilege when you killed two people and were sentenced to life in prison without the possibility of parole. Session dismissed. Jennifer Long, inmate 264290, please come back with a better attitude. Guard!"

Chapter Twenty-four

Aaliyah

"Eron," she yelled as soon as she opened the door. Aaliyah was pissed that he parked in the middle of the driveway. It left no room for her to get her car into the driveway. Aaliyah was very strategic with her steps with her being in pain twenty-four seven.

"Why the fuck is it so dark in here?" Aaliyah snapped, turning on the light in the foyer. She was PMSing, so every little thing was pissing her off. "Let me relax," she tried to tell herself as she locked the door.

"Oh. My. God."

As if on cue, Eric Benét's "Spend My Life with You" came on.

"Aaliyah, I just want you to come dance with me. Can you do that?" Eron extended his hand for Aaliyah to grasp.

"Yes." Eron held on to Aaliyah ever so gracefully. Aaliyah's legs were bad as she couldn't dance for real, but they couldn't sing for shit. But they held a tune, singing to each other.

I never knew such a day could come, and I never knew such a love could be inside of one.

"Damn. That's my shit."

"I know, right?"

"Sit down. I know you're a trooper. But I also know your legs hurt."

"So bad. I didn't want to ruin the mood though."

"See, hearing shit like that lets me know I'm doing the right thing. You make this shit easy. Come in the backyard," Eron said all in one breath.

Aaliyah had never seen Eron nervous, so it was making her nervous about what she thought he was trying to get the courage to do. She didn't want to get to ahead of herself, so she was just following his lead. Truthfully, even if this didn't lead to a proposal, she'd be happy, because he'd never done anything this nice and intimate.

"Close your eyes."

Aaliyah felt Eron leave her side, so her balance shifted.

"Now open them," she heard Eron yell from a distance.

Aaliyah just stood still as Eron stood in the middle of their family and friends. Each person held a sign that read: WILL YOU MARRY THIS GUY? There were even arrows pointing to him as stood there in his B-boy stance.

"I have a letter I want to read you. Aaliyah," Eron announced, pulling out his phone.

"Well, that's romantic!" somebody from the crowd shouted, making everybody snicker. It was almost as if joke was just what the doctor ordered.

"I'll e-mail it to her when I'm done. But anyway, this will be short and sweet."

"Damn, dog, she really gon' say no now," Jamal whispered in a genuinely sad tone loud enough so everybody could hear him.

"Mal, shut up, stupid," Aaliyah snapped jokingly.

Dear Aaliyah,
The last time you wrote a letter, it was sad. I was hoping this one could replace that one. I love you. I knew you were special when I saw you get tested over and over. The doctor came out preparing me for death, but we believed otherwise. Every day,

*seeing you push through makes me fall in love
all over again. Your selflessness is infectious. The
list goes on and on, but I know that I start to feel
cheated with you only being my girl. I need you to
be my wife.*

*Aaliyah, I know you never wanted a big wedding.
I just wanted to make you feel special. Will you
marry me?*

Eron stood in front of Aaliyah, looking goofy.

"Son, get on your knee." His mother dragged him from
his nervousness.

Aaliyah stood there, crying and shaking her head.

Dior shouted, "We can't hear you!"

Eron dropped to his knee and slid the Leo diamond
engagement one-carat, round-cut, $14,000 white gold
ring onto her finger.

Chapter Twenty-five

Tineya

Tineya was truly living her best life. She'd just sat on her couch to catch up on some reality TV when her phone rang.

"Ugggghhh! Tineya."

"Yes, Dior. What's wrong?"

"This baby is kicking my ass, and his or her father is stupid."

Yes, Dior and Mal were expecting a baby. He was a rare breed. He loved him some Dior. That man didn't give a fuck about what happened to her as a child, what she did before him, or nothing. Actually, it became more of a struggle for Dior. She dodged him for as long as she could. She didn't want to deal with him for fear of him rejecting her. She would always say that one day he would pick up and decide that he would judge her on her past indiscretions.

One day, they all sat around drinking and ended up playing truth or dare? By some stroke of luck, which had to be God, it was on Dior and Mal.

"Truth or dare, Jamal?" said Dior.

"Truth."

The room was quiet, watching the exchange. "Could you be with somebody you knew was promiscuous?" she asked.

"Depends on who she is."

"Figures."

Mal scooted his chair back roughly. He grabbed Dior's arm. *"Aye, let me talk to you for a minute."*

Dior went along with him.

"Aye, my man, we gon' be in the basement."

"You got it," Eron said smoothly, while Aaliyah sat with her lip tooted up like something stank.

Downstairs, Mal said to Dior, *"You gon' quit trying me in front of people. Let me answer your question. If I'm feeling the woman, then I don't care what kind of past she has. But one thing I do like is confidence. I need her to stand on any decisions she's made thus far."*

"But what are you doing though?" Dior asked. Fuck him. He ain't no damn body! *Dior tried to convince herself.*

Mal began to walk in Dior's direction, yanking his shirt over his head. Dior gasped, watching him walk over to her. It might've been one of the sexiest moments ever. He walked toward her with his wife beater hugging his pecks. His Bally's belt hung loosely, swinging as he walked. His boxer briefs were slightly visible. Mal held his pants as if he was grabbing his dick.

"Now, what you say?" Mal asked as he stood abs to chest with Dior.

"I said, what the fuck are you doing?" Dior retorted, seemingly unbothered. She gulped right after, or she attempted to, but her mouth came up dry.

"Oh, what am I doing, huh?"

Dior chuckled.

"Earlier you just wanted me all up in that pussy! You played a dangerous game asking them grown-woman questions. What up now?" he stated adamantly, causing Dior to cringe.

"Dawg, will you grow the fuck up!" Mal added, and they both laughed.

"So, what? You know I hate the sound of pussy because it sounds nasty and wet and juicy! Ugh!"

Dior was still laughing and went about things as if he weren't even there. But Mal knew better. She wanted him at all costs, but she didn't want to seem too eager.

Mal moved around Dior's body so arrogantly. It was familiar territory to him. Mal didn't know it, but when the stresses of the streets became too much for him, he ran to Dior. She was his dawg! She was his ride or die, and she didn't even know it.

She was tired of playing with Mal. The gesture of him answering that question all daddyish had her. Dior didn't care that they were going about things backward.

"Umm." Dior let go of a soft moan as she started to rub her sweet spot as Mal's dick rubbed up against her legs.

"So you gon' act like you don't see me, huh? You are something else." Mal leaned her over the couch, fucking her senseless. That was the day that Dior got pregnant.

"Dior!"

"Ummm, what?"

"Girl, I just had a flashback of the time when we all played truth or dare? Remember I showed y'all the tape?"

Eron's and Aaliyah's freaky asses had the tape rolling from a previous rendezvous.

"Okay, bye, Dior. Somebody at my door. I'ma call you right back."

"Who is that? Ro?"

"Get out of my business." Click.

Tineya watched as Ro stepped out of his car. Ro and Tineya had formed a genuine friendship. After they left the house, he went with her to the lawyer.

Her uncle Nathan had been saying he was helping her, but that was the furthest thing from the truth. When she went to see the lawyer, he had been looking for her. Nathan forged initially Nick's signature, basically saying that he was the overseer. So while he was playing like he was looking out, Tineya was actually taking care of him.

It was Ro who recommended she take the paperwork to her own attorney. Nick even left some cash in the safe. Even in death, her parents were making sure she was good.

"What's up?" Ro's fine ass stepped into the house, hugging Tineya around the waist and kissing her face directly on her scar.

Tineya leaned her head into the kiss. Ro used his other hand to rub down Tineya's body.

"Umm." Tineya's body disobeyed her when it released that moan. She hadn't had sex in a nice little while.

"You know we don't gotta do this, right?" Ro questioned.

"What, you don't want to?" Tineya took a step back.

"Don't step back. I want it. You fine as hell. I like everything about you. I want you to be sure you are sure 'cause ain't no coming back."

"This is what I want."

"Okay. Come on." Ro grabbed her hand, dropping his basketball shorts along the way.

Ro immediately went to rubbing Tineya's nipple on down. Ro felt her breathing begin to change. He noticed that the farther he went down, the quicker Tineya's breathing had become. Ro knew she wanted some oral by the way she ground her hot box into him. Ro, using his tongue, made a wet trail down the center of Tineya's body. He used his hands to touch whatever parts his tongue missed. She couldn't believe it. He had her seeing stars, and he hadn't even gotten to the nitty-gritty.

"Oh. Shit!" Ro continued to use his tongue to trace the triangular shape. Ro was eye level with Tineya's clit. It was hooded. Ro pulled the hood back. He wanted to see what kind of clit Tineya was hiding. He already liked her bald pussy. The lips were tight and intact.

"Damn!" Ro couldn't help but voice his pleasure. His mouth watered at the sight. Ro knew a secret about women. He was smart enough to know that sex wasn't "one size fits all." Just because you did it one way to one woman didn't mean that would work for another woman. He didn't mind taking the time to learn and listen to a woman's body if she was worth it.

Ro proceeded to use his extremely wet mouth to assault her clit. He kissed it. He licked it. He firmly pressed his two inner fingers on it as if it were a button. He placed it between his thumb and index finger, rubbing in a circular motion.

"Oh my Gawd. Shit!" Tineya was losing it. The way she gripped the sheets, causing ash to build up at the knuckle, was a natural reaction of pleasure.

"Nah, I ain't done until you are." Ro was serious. Tineya tried pulling away for a breather, but he wasn't having that. He took pleasure in seeing Tineya in a pure form. It was all sexy to him. The way she fought to prove her attraction to him. The way she lay with her torso lifted off the bed. The wet puddle forming was all real for Ro. He wasn't letting up. Ro wanted Tineya to know that in all this time, he saw her. In no time, Tineya was screaming out for her release.

"Rooo." Tineya attempted to scream Ro's name, but the way she was cumming had her in a daze. Ro watched it all, rubbing on his dick. He was more than prepared for Tineya's wet walls to grip his dick like a suction cup. Not even air was getting in.

"Oh shit! This can't be real. This shit good as hell." Tineya's pussy had Ro dazed.

"Wait, wait, wait. Can we just sit here for a second?" Tineya asked, attempting to hold Ro in that spot. He was feeling her completely.

Ro made eye contact with Tineya. It was at that point that he knew he had fucked up.

"I'm sorry, baby. I can't sit in this and not do nothing with it," Ro replied, looking at her for confirmation to go on. Waiting took every bit of Ro's composure. When she gave him the slightest nod, he began to stroke. Ro went through a range of meaningless thoughts to keep himself from ejaculating too soon. He didn't want to let her down. He knew how she felt about him.

"Umm."

"Damn, man."

The two lost it. Their moans and grunts took over the room. Ro took up storage in Tineya's pussy for about twenty minutes. Ro pulled his penis out slowly. His dick was much too tender for any fast movement.

Tineya was too comfortable lying in Ro's embrace. She chose to ignore Ro smirking.

"You not fooling anybody. You not asleep. Your breathing pattern isn't labored enough for you to be asleep."

Tineya couldn't help but laugh at his inquisitive mind. Only Ro would pay attention to someone's breathing pattern.

Ro lay there as he kissed Tineya's scar. Tineya wasn't sure how things were going to play out, but this was effortless and unique. Life was what it was.

Coming soon . . .

Tales of a D-Girl

Chapter One

*Like a G, I hold it down for the town I'm at. In a flash
like that, recognize I'm back.*

"Hey!" Keyana sang. They were playing T.I., her favorite artist, as soon as she and Alyssa walked into the
District 81 party at the Whitney. Alyssa was smiling and
shaking her head because she already knew when they
played T.I. anywhere Keyana was at, she was going crazy,
flowing word for word. He was definitely her favorite
entertainer. That was just something you were going to
have to accept about her.

This was a District 81 party, so it was a nice, laidback
crowd. These were grown men, professional men, foot-
ball-playing men, basketball-playing men, so Keyana and
Alyssa were in true heaven. Real street niggas were in the
building also. I mean, not niggas that were street niggas
by relation, but niggas who had that "get money" shit in
their blood.

Keyana and Alyssa were on summer break from Ferris
State University. Since they were going back to school
the following day, they wanted to make their last twenty-four hours home memorable. Detroit was their home-
town. They loved it. There was nothing like the D to them.
They decided on this day that they were straight wilding
out, showing a nigga some shit he ain't ever seen before.
Keyana and Alyssa had a "fuck it" attitude naturally.
That's how Detroit made most of its residents.

They were both buzzing from the pre-drink at Alyssa's cousin's house, so they were feeling nice. So, to the bar they went, to get that one more drink to get them right. They were both beautiful, dressed like true divas. Alyssa had pretty brown blemish-free skin. Her big, brown eyes were most guys' weakness about her, if they had to choose one. Her lips were big and smooth. She never ever wore lip gloss, just Chapstick. On Alyssa's five feet one inch frame she wore a see-through top with a brown bra underneath, allowing her C-cups to salute, with the black short shorts covering a small portion of her medium-thick thighs. Lugged sole booties adorned her manicured feet. Her hair stayed done. Matter of fact, she and Keyana had just left from Mike's chair at Salon DNA over on Detroit's west side earlier that day. The timepiece she chose for the night was a Joe Rodeo, with a chain that hung right between her breasts with a square diamond pendant and matching earrings. She finished off her outfit with a brown Damier clutch by Louis Vuitton.

Suddenly, out of nowhere, the finest guy Keyana had ever seen jumped in front of her at the bar. "Excuse me!" Keyana shouted with her lethal tongue, in more ways than one. She rolled her eyes as she thought that this perfect stranger may be the perfect candidate for tonight.

"Oh my bad, baby. I didn't even see you standing there."

Keyana gave him a smile for three reasons: he was fine, she was fucking him tonight, and she knew he was lying about not seeing her.

Keyana was nowhere near conceited, but confident she was. With her dark brown complexion, she was so pretty. She even had a few blemishes that men never seemed to notice. Her eyes were big with long eyelashes. She had pouty lips and a nice-size nose. Her breasts were only a B-cup, but they were sitting erect in her low-cut lace sleeveless purple top that fell right at the top of her ass.

She had ass for days, so you know it looked good in her gold ribbed leggings. She wore a simple gold necklace. For shoes, she wore peep-toe pumps that were purple with gold trimming. So again he couldn't have meant what he said about not noticing her!

"Baby, I don't take kindly to people laughing in my face," Mr. Fine replied with a smile forming and stepping in her personal space.

"I'm sorry, but you should stop cracking jokes," Keyana responded. Normally Keyana would have been mad at the stranger's arrogance and stepped back, but instead, she took her time looking him up and down. From a quick glance, she could tell he had on a Louis Vuitton outfit and a chunky wristwatch. For the whole two minutes, this stranger kept her captivated by his presence. She hadn't looked for Alyssa. Finally, she looked over to her right, and there was Alyssa all giddy in front of this fine specimen. She gave Alyssa a wink. It was then that she noticed that the bar stranger and Alyssa's friend knew each other, which was a plus in her book and the game plan.

"What's your name, baby?" Mr. Fine asked, bringing her attention back to him.

"Keyana."

"Beautiful, Keyana. Can I buy you a drink since I cut in front of you in line?"

"Yes, please."

"Polite, too? Will you marry me?"

"Can I know your name first?"

"Brice, but you can call me B."

"I bet everyone calls you B huh? I want to call you Brice, if you don't mind."

"Oh, you're trying to be separated from everyone else huh?"

"Yes, sir, you're learning."

They stood there engrossed in each other so long that Keyana didn't notice she didn't get her drink. She looked at her iPhone to check the time. It was 1:50 a.m. Alyssa and her friend were walking toward them.

"Kevin, this is my best friend, Keyana."

"Hi, Keyana. I see my boy B been keeping you hostage, huh?" Kevin said, introducing himself with a joke.

"Hey, Ms. Alyssa," Brice spoke, not wanting to be rude.

"Hi, B."

Keyana stepped back, causing her to really look at Brice. He was gorgeous. He was about six foot two and wasn't overly cocky, but his broad shoulders let you know that he wasn't a stranger to the gym. She had to have them sexy-ass lips that blocked a beautiful set of pearly whites. They looked smoke free. His eyes were hazel. In addition, his hair was curly in a low-cut taper. Keyana saw that the guys were engaged in a conversation, while Alyssa was sitting with the same glazed look she just had, only she was staring at Kevin.

Alyssa took his looks in. She stared at Kevin's light skin and light brown, almost see-through eyes. His curly hair too was in a taper. He had light freckles over his nose. He was cocky in build. Keyana knew B, from all indications, wouldn't be the only one getting some pussy tonight. Keyana felt Brice grabbing her hand, and she looked over at him.

"You zoned out on me for a minute. I hope I was the reason your mind was gone," he stated, hoping for the best.

"You'll never know, Brice," Keyana replied, smiling and sticking her tongue out as enticingly as she could. *I will have this nigga where I want him in no time,* Keyana thought knowingly.

"You better keep that tongue in your mouth!" Brice replied with a serious look. It was sexy, too. His voice even dropped an octave.

"Whatever." Keyana's nasty mind was wandering all over the place at what she could do with her tongue.

Brice leaned over, taking a deep breath to ask a question. "Would I be too forward if I told you I wanted to take you to the room and do something to you?"

Keyana couldn't take it. The combination of his minty breath on her neck and his deep baritone was just too much for her. She sat there for a minute. *I'm here from school. I want some dick from his fine ass. Alyssa and I said that we were on some Lil Wayne shit and giving someone their "one night only."* She glanced at Brice, knowing that he would be the one to fulfill her fantasy of wanting to have sex with the possibility of being caught. Her phone vibrated with a text from Alyssa.

Fuckin him 2nite. Lol & u betta do B fine ass, text ya wit the room #

Keyana looked up just in time to see Alyssa waving with a goofy smile. Keyana sent a reply.

Hell yeah, fuck it, safe sex tho! LoL b careful & don't 4get text u the same.

Keyana leaned over, whispering, "What are we waiting on?" Brice looked shocked but grabbed her hand and kissed her on the cheek. "I drove my car," Keyana expressed.

"Follow me to MGM," Brice replied, walking her to her Impala, which just so happened to be parked in the same lot as his black Range Rover Sport.

Keyana sat contemplating for a minute. *I don't know anything about this man!* She almost talked herself out of it. *My adrenaline is pumping though.* She continued her one-person debate. Her scattered thoughts turned her on so much that her hand found its way into her leggings, where her juices were pouring out. She was soaking wet!

As Brice consumed her thoughts, she totally forgot that he was following her. She pulled over on a dark one-way street, pulled her pants down over her ass, opened her legs as wide as she could, and began rotating her fingers over her clit. She was moaning, thinking about Brice's tongue gently licking her clit. She began to get louder with each stroke. There was a knock on the window followed by a yank on the door handle. Keyana looked to her left, and there was Brice staring at her with them seductive eyes.

"I see you can't wait. You ain't got to! Let me help you. Open the door." After she unlocked the door, Brice grabbed both of her legs, turning her around so her feet were outside the car. But her feet never touched the ground because Brice threw them over his shoulders. He was still tall on his knees, so he had to pick up the pussy, bringing it to his mouth like a dinner plate. Keyana's eyes were closed, so she was shocked when she felt his mouth on her pussy. Brice should have warned her he was a "Head Doctor." He looked up at her, and she made some of the sexiest faces he had ever seen. No part of her pussy went untouched. He licked her with skill.

"Shit, B, I can't take it!" Keyana screamed, trying to run.

"Oh, now I'm B, huh?" Brice asked, being sarcastic. "Your pussy tastes so good." He continuously licked up and down her slit, opening her pussy and going straight to the clit. That was all she wrote because shortly after Brice knew she was at the point of no return.

"I'm cumming!" Keyana announced breathlessly.

Brice knew she was cumming. He felt her clit harden under his tongue. He felt her juices on his lips, so he opened his mouth so that he could drink all of her. "Umm!" Brice sang as he swallowed. "You think we can make it to the room, nasty?" he inquired jokingly as Keyana lay there trying to control her breathing.

"No, I'm not done with you yet!" Keyana exclaimed. This was her fantasy so she couldn't let him ruin it. Brice didn't know it, but he was an innocent bystander in Keyana's encounter. She got up, pulling him by his belt buckle, and she started unbuckling it. She unzipped his pants, pulling out what was already pointing at her. His dick was so big and pretty. It was a natural reaction for her to deep throat him.

"Oh shit, girl, hold up!" Brice tried to stop her, but she wouldn't let up. He was moaning more than she had, and she loved it. Watching that movie with Superhead and Mr. Marcus paid off! Once Keyana saw that tape and how Superhead had badass Mr. Marcus running, she vowed to learn to make a nigga act like that. Keyana started to slow down with the deep throat. She started to tickle the head of his dick with her tongue. He went crazy. "Oh my . . . Shit. Damn, I love me a Detroit bitch!" Brice admitted.

Keyana didn't mind. She knew her head game was on fire. She also knew that they didn't make many females like her. She'd mastered that head shit. Keyana laid her tongue flat, opening her mouth as wide as she could so that he could fuck her face. Keyana grabbed his hand, placing it on the back of her head. He fucked her face. She took that shit though, and in no time at all, Keyana knew he would be cumming.

"Shit, I'm about to cum. You gon' catch it, Key?" Brice requested, hoping that she would oblige.

Keyana began sucking harder, feeling his dick pulsate as he began cumming. He shot straight to the back of her throat, and she immediately began swallowing while jacking him off. She kept going to the last drop.

"Shit. Damn!" Brice yelled. He was trying not to, but it came out.

Keyana giggled. "You all right, Brice?"

"Damn! I'm good."

Keyana got up and opened her purse and pulled out a gold wrapper. She then went and gave him one more hard suck to get him to his full potential. All Brice could say was, "Damn."

Keyana got him right and opened the condom, putting it on with her mouth, and she stood up. She went to the front of his Range, bending over and making her booty clap. She could see his lustful eyes in the dark as he walked over to her while jacking off a little bit. Keyana felt him start to enter her, causing her knees to almost give out on her. Brice then wrapped his arm around her waist for more leverage.

"Um. Um!" Keyana released a light moan that heightened his arousal.

Brice was a smart guy, so for a minute, he kept sliding in and out just to hear that particular moan. Brice was shocked at how tight she was. He couldn't help trying to figure out why Keyana's pussy was so tight.

"You are going to make me cum, B!" Keyana stated as audibly as she could.

"I like when you call me B," Brice responded in a lustful voice as he continued to stroke her.

"Oh yes, um." Keyana couldn't stop moaning. He felt so good to her. His strokes were professional almost. He was hitting all corners at all angles. He found her G-spot in no time.

Something has to be wrong with this girl. This shit too good to be true, he thought. So, Brice was more than surprised when he felt her start to throw that shit back. She was taking control. He just stood back and held her hips. "Damn, girl, you throwing that ass back, doing all that moaning. Your pussy is the shit though. Damn and this shit so fuckin' tight!" She might have had some of the best pussy he ever had. The tingling he felt let him know that he was moments away from cumming. Keyana was thinking the same thing about him. She just knew a Higher Being made this dick just for her girl. "I'm trying to hold out, but this pussy won't let me!"

They had been going at it for about thirty-five minutes, so Keyana was more than good. She felt it anyway. She was ready. "I'm ready to cum on your big dick," Keyana panted.

That was it. Brice knew it. He started going really fast and hard. Keyana was getting louder by the second.

"I'm cumming, B, shit!" Brice was too.

"Fuck!" Brice exclaimed as he began to shake. In no time, he collapsed on Keyana's juicy ass. They just lay there in silence for a few minutes.

Brice wasted no time giving her praises for their encounter. He was beyond mesmerized. "Damn, girl, your sex is amazing. Never in my twenty-five years on this earth have I had pussy with head that good. You wasn't playing, you wasn't lazy, and you was throwing that shit back. Damn!"

Keyana just sat looking at him with a lazy grin. "Well thank you! What can I say? I'm a D-Girl!"

"G'on ahead and get your laughing out. You got the right to be arrogant, and that's what I'ma call you. D-Girl." Brice had her blushing.

"With a dick that big, you can call me whatever you like." Keyana zoned out for a minute. *Damn, do I just get in my car and leave like nothing happened? Do I tell him that this was only a one-time thing? Fuck it, I would be crazy not to fuck again and get the fuck on.*

"You over there looking real confused," Brice responded. "Look, I'm tired as hell. Let's just get a room tonight and worry about tomorrow, tomorrow."

Chapter Two

Brice whipped the Range like it was a little Ne-Ne (Neon). They were there in literally two minutes. Brice paid the valet for both cars, and together they walked in. Keyana stood off to the side to give him some space so he wouldn't catch her looking at his money. Some niggas tried to stunt on you by pulling out their money. Keyana wasn't giving him the satisfaction.

"Hello, sir. It's a great day at MGM Grand Hotel. What can I do for you?" said the perky white girl with big tits and blond hair.

"Hi. I'll just take a luxury room."

"Okay, great. May I see a form of ID? And will you be using a credit card or cash?"

"Credit," Brice said.

Keyana was more than surprised when he pulled out a black American Express card. The perky white girl got excited too. Keyana didn't care though. It was what it was. But one thing for sure, two things for certain, Keyana was not leaving that hotel without some money.

"Okay, Mr. Johnson, here is your key card along with your ID. Just take the elevator to your left to the tenth floor, and your room number is 1019."

"Thank you," Brice answered gathering the things she had given him. "Come on, Key," Brice said, turning around and then realizing that Keyana was already walking toward the elevator. Brice caught up with her, and together they got on the elevator.

"Look, I just want you to know that I like you. You seem cool, and I'ma look out for you. Now, don't take that the wrong way. Shit, just like you a D-Girl, baby, I'm a D-Boy to the core. I look out for people who look out for me."

Brice was interrupted when the elevator alerted them that they were on the tenth floor. Brice took a deep breath, walking down to the room and opening the door. Neither one of them looked at the room in awe because neither one was new to the MGM. "Like I was saying, I'm a Detroit nigga. I'ma be blunt with you. I'm a nigga on the go. I don't have time to be dating. Most of the time a nigga just wants to fuck. So I appreciate this shit more than you know."

Keyana sat there with the same blank look she had on the elevator. She was in awe at his honesty. She appreciated it. She was a master at disguise, because in her head she was happy that he wouldn't be a tough egg to crack. They were on the same shit. Just like Rick Ross said: *Every moment thinking money. I bust a nut then I'm back to thinking money*

Keyana gave a little smirk. "In no way do I take anything you saying in a bad way. I'm glad you realize that fair exchange ain't robbery. Don't get me wrong, I don't need shit. It's just the principle."

Keyana took a deep breath, realizing that she hadn't heard from Alyssa. She fumbled with her purse until she found her phone. There were two texts from Alyssa.

Where u, bitch?

MGM 921. I'm 'bout 2 put a Missing Person Report.

Keyana giggled as she texted Alyssa back.

I'm good. MGM 1019. 'bout 2, ready n hr.

Alyssa had to be waiting by the phone because she replied almost instantly.

K, my phone loud. Hit me.

Keyana knew Alyssa wouldn't be texting back, so she looked at Brice patiently waiting. "So, are we good?" Keyana inquired. She got up so that she was between his legs. She began unbuttoning her shirt. As if they were magnetically drawn, his hands went straight to her hips.

"Yeah, we good, Key. I'm tryin'a hear you call me B again," Brice said, laughing. He thought it was weird how she already adapted to calling him B while they were sexing.

Keyana couldn't help laughing as she removed his hands from her hips, stepping back to give Brice a strip tease. She was tired as hell, but she had to get that potent dick and lethal tongue again because after that she was gone. She didn't have a man, so she wanted a nigga like Jeezy, "slam dunking in the pussy, and not laying up." She ran her hands over each shoulder, letting her shirt fall to the floor. Immediately, her hand went to her breasts, taking the time to caress her nipples. Brice let out a deep breath as he pulled off his jeans. She stepped back, bending all the way over and sliding her leggings down as she went all the way to the floor. She turned around to give him ass shot stepping out of the leggings.

She doesn't have on any panties.

Keyana saw the look of shock on his face. By the time Keyana made it to the bathroom, she was completely naked. Brice was right behind her, snatching his shirt off. Keyana adjusted the water and got in the shower with Brice on her heels. Keyana wanted to at least wash up after their little rendezvous, but Brice had other plans. He backed her up to the wall of the shower, grabbed her face and kissing her. It surprised the both of them. It was so passionate the intensity was overwhelming. Their hunger for each other spoke volumes. From there he made one long lick to her collarbone. He grabbed each of her breasts and began going back and forth between the two with firm bites and soft kisses.

"Shit, um!" Keyana's moans grew hungrier as she began running her hands through his curly hair. Brice loved that shit. He skipped her whole stomach to grab both of her legs, throwing them over his shoulder. He handled her like she was small. He loved the way her thick, soft thighs felt on his face. That shit turned her on. "Wait. Wait, shit. I'm about to cum." Brice wouldn't believe it if he didn't feel her tense up. He had her creaming in no time. "Fuck, shit, B." Keyana deflated right in his arms.

They both laughed. Keyana got herself together quick. She got up, turned him around, and dropped to her knees. Mike, her stylist, would be pissed because her hair was ruined. Keyana showed Brice no mercy. His dick was so big. She went up and down on it as fast as she could. Keyana looked up at him as she sucked. The combination of the water sliding down her body and her ass sticking out was too much for him.

"Damn, girl, shit, hold up!" Brice couldn't take it. He began trying to back up, but he had nowhere to go. Keyana knew she could get him there in no time. She felt him begin to pulsate in her mouth. "Damn, Key, I'm not ready!" Brice gasped.

Keyana began to suck harder and tickle the head with her tongue. She went up and down as fast as she could while jacking him off.

"Shit!" Brice moaned. Brice looked down at her. Keyana held his eye contact as she held her mouth open to catch as much nut as she could. She even stroked him one last time to squeeze out the last drop, and she swallowed it all. Great head was hard to find in the streets, and tight pussy seemed nonexistent these days. *This bitch is amazing.* Once Keyana swallowed, she started right back to sucking. "Damn," Brice said, astonished at her stamina.

In no time Brice was back hard. Keyana stood up, grabbing his hand and leading him to the bed. As Brice got comfortable, she went to her purse and ripped the condom wrapper off, sliding it on his dick.

Keyana looked at Brice and said, "You ready for me to ride?"

"Yeah, I'm ready, Key," Brice said in that low, sexy, deep voice she fell in love with.

Keyana slid down on his dick slow, her pussy gripping him every step of the way. She had to adjust herself to his size. "Ahhhh," Keyana groaned while Brice's eyes rolled in the back of his head.

"Shit!" Brice shouted.

Keyana just sat for a minute. She could cum just from sitting there. Having sex for the first time with anyone was usually awkward, but they were in sync sexually. They didn't have a timid moment. It was like they were made to fuck each other. Keyana began to ride. She went slowly at first. Brice gripped her ass so he could go deeper.

"Wait, B, shit. I feel you in my stomach!" Keyana declared in a low, sexy moan that drove Brice wild, making him want to stay deep. Keyana took it like a champ. Whoever said thick girls couldn't take dick didn't know Keyana. Keyana found her groove. She wanted Brice to feel everything. She went around and around and sped up, and the way he caressed her hips drove her wild. "Uh. Um. Uh, shit, yeah!" Keyana was moaning loudly. She tried to contain herself, but the dick was too good. She wasn't the only one who was loud. Brice let go too.

"Damn, Key, this pussy so good, and you riding this muthafucka!" Brice just watched her hips go around and around on his dick, causing him to become mesmerized. He watched her abs caving in and out as she went in circles on his dick. "Damn, this is the shit, Key!" Brice yelled.

"Um. Um, B, shit, um, this dick is so damn good," Keyana moaned.

"Key, I want to see you cum. Can you do that for me?"

"B, I don't know." Keyana didn't quite understand what he meant.

Brice looked her dead in her eyes, answering, "I'ma make you!" Brice leaned up, grabbing her legs and placing them on his forearm. He lifted her all the way off his dick and then slammed her all the way down on it.

"Umm. Umm!" Keyana started going crazy.

Brice did it again and again. He went deep one last time, pulling most of his dick out, leaving the head in and watching her cream down his dick. "Yeah, that's what I wanted to see. Key, look!"

Keyana wanted to look down, she even tried, but she was shaking too bad. "Umm, shit, B, damn, fuck!" Keyana went crazy as Brice stuck his dick all the way back in and kept fucking her.

"Damn, girl. Shit. You are wet as hell!" Brice uttered.

Keyana knew she had to show him something because right now he was in the lead. Keyana pushed him on his back so that he could lie flat. She started off fast and then went slow, winding her midsection like she was hip rolling. "Damn, Key, umm!" Brice was slowly losing control. Keyana placed each foot flat on the bed. She lifted up slightly, going around and around on his dick. "Damn, straight up, Key? Work that shit! Fuck!" Brice responded in a low, husky voice. Keyana put her feet behind her knees flat on the bed, turning around to the reverse cowgirl position. Trina said it best: *I can spin around and keep the dick still inside.* Keyana went all the way down on the dick, straightening her back so that her breasts were on his legs. She began making her ass clap all over his abs. Brice was in shock. All he could do was moan and lightly rub her ass. "Damn, Key, bounce that shit!" he hollered. Out of nowhere, she started going up and down on his dick. Brice was ready. "Key, I'ma bust!" Brice alerted her.

"Cum on. I'm ready too!" Keyana replied softly. She felt Brice tighten up, and his dick grew in width and length. Keyana could barely contain herself. "Um. Um. Damn, it's too big!" Keyana shouted.

"Here I cum, Key," Brice announced. Brice gripped Keyana's ass as he came hard.

"Damn!" Keyana took a deep breath.

Silence filled the room. It wasn't an awkward silence but a fulfilled one. Neither Brice nor Keyana moved a muscle.